As they approached the final bend, Maxine was still within striking distance of the leading group. Th̶e̶r̶e̶ ̶w̶a̶s̶ ̶a̶ ̶b̶r̶i̶e̶f̶ entered the final straight when she thought that she might be able to overtake all of them, surprising them down the outside, but then, suddenly, they were running away from her as Hiari accelerated explosively and the others responded.

There was nothing Maxine could do but watch as Jade moved past Hui Zhong and Jerry and almost caught Hiari on the line. Maxine finished fifth, with Martha nearly catching her. She had run as fast as she knew how, but it hadn't been good enough . . .

Don't miss the first title in the *Camp Gold* series
by Christine Ohuruogu:

CAMP GOLD: RUNNING STARS

CAMP GOLD

GOING FOR GOLD

Christine Ohuruogu

with Paul May

Tamarind Books

CAMP GOLD: GOING FOR GOLD 978 1 848 53094 2
A TAMARIND BOOK

First published in Great Britain by Tamarind Books,
an imprint of Random House Children's Publishers UK
A Random House Group Company

Tamarind Books edition published 2012

1 3 5 7 9 10 8 6 4 2

The Random House Group Limited supports the Forest Stewardship Council (FSC®),
the leading international forest certification organization. Our books carrying the FSC label are printed
on FSC®-certified paper. FSC is the only forest certification scheme endorsed by the leading environmental
organizations, including Greenpeace. Our paper procurement policy can be found at
www.randomhouse.co.uk/environment.

MIX
Paper from
responsible sources
FSC® C016897

Set in Bembo

Tamarind Books are published by Random House Children's Publishers UK
61–63 Uxbridge Road, London W5 5SA

www.**randomhousechildrens**.co.uk
www.**totallyrandombooks**.co.uk
www.**tamarindbooks**.co.uk

Addresses for companies within The Random House Group Limited can be found at:
www.randomhouse.co.uk/offices.htm

THE RANDOM HOUSE GROUP Limited Reg. No. 954009

A CIP catalogue record for this book is available from the British Library.

Printed and bound in Great Britain by CPI Group (UK) Ltd, Croydon, CR0 4YY

For Mum, Dad, Obi, Charles, Victoria, Daniel,
Kingsley, Gabriel and Joshua.

CHAPTER ONE

'There they are!' yelled Maxine. 'I see them!
Come on, Mum, please hurry!'

Maxine was with her mum and her little
brother, Joshua. The train ride to the airport had
seemed to take for ever, and now Maxine's mum
was gazing up at the overhead information board
trying to find the flight to Barcelona. But
Maxine could already see her friend Sasha, the
fiery red-haired Russian pole-vaulter, waving

madly at her from the other side of the massive glass-and-steel departure hall.

The invitation to be a part of Camp Gold International had dropped through the letterbox a month ago, and Maxine still couldn't quite believe it was happening. She tugged again at her mother's arm. 'There's no need to look up there,' she said impatiently. 'They're all here. I can see John, and Michael. Oh, wow! There's Danny Crowe too. I wonder if he's coming with us. Hey, Mum, will you please hurry?'

'All right,' said her mother with a smile. 'There's no harm in making sure now, is there? You go on ahead with Joshua and I'll bring the bags.'

'Thanks, Mum.' Maxine gave her mother a hug, grabbed Joshua's hand and zig-zagged off through the crowd to join her friends.

Sasha screamed with excitement, hugged Maxine and threw Joshua up into the air. 'This is so fantastic!' she said. 'We are all together again. We will have the most amazing time.'

'Not all of us,' said Maxine a little sadly. 'There are no gymnasts at this camp, so Kayle couldn't come.'

Kayle was Maxine's oldest friend and she had been with them at the very first Camp Gold the summer before. Maxine and Kayle had both been selected for Camp Gold as gymnasts, but Maxine had discovered that she had a talent for running. She would be fourteen in September, and after a year of hard work she was now one of the top junior 800-metre runners in the country. Sasha was right: going to Camp Gold International was going to be amazing, but it was a shame that Kayle wouldn't be there too. Still, Maxine thought with a smile, Kayle would be having a great time with the other gymnasts. They were all returning to the awesome Camp Gold site by the sea where so much had happened last year.

'Hi, Maxine,' said a gruff voice from behind her.

Maxine turned and saw John. At least, she thought it was John. The tall, tough-looking boy definitely had John's grin and his sparkling blue eyes, but this boy was about a foot taller than he'd been the last time Maxine had seen him.

'I know,' said John, shaking Maxine's hand enthusiastically. 'I've kind of grown, haven't I? But that's good, because my times have gotten a whole lot better.'

'And that's why you're here,' said Michael Gladstone as he joined them. Michael was the principal of Camp Gold. 'You guys have all kept on improving and now you're going to be up against the best in the world.'

Maxine shivered with excitement. It was true: a year ago she hadn't even known that she could be a runner. Now she was heading off to an international camp where she would be running against other athletes from all around the world. It was thrilling beyond words.

A tall and very beautiful young woman had her arm linked through Michael's, and suddenly Maxine saw the gleam of a gold ring on her finger. 'Isabel!' she exclaimed. 'You're married!'

Isabel had been the head gymnastics coach at Camp Gold the year before and the friends had watched her romance with Michael from a distance. Maxine was thrilled. If Camp Gold International was half as interesting as Camp Gold had been they would be in for an incredible three weeks.

'Does this mean you're coming too?' Maxine asked Isabel.

'You bet,' she replied. 'We only got married two days ago. I'm not letting him out of my sight.'

'And I'm coming too,' said Danny Crowe. 'It'll be good to get away from all the publicity for a few weeks. Plus, I tweaked a hamstring in that race last week. I need a break.'

Danny was a four-times Olympic gold medallist who had been an inspiration to the young athletes at Camp Gold. He had been a lot of fun too. And just a week ago he had won yet another gold medal for the 400 metres at the World Championships.

'Is that why you're wearing dark glasses?' laughed Sasha. 'So you can avoid the photographers? It hasn't worked very well.'

Maxine looked round and saw a small throng of press photographers heading directly towards them. 'I'm sorry, Danny,' Michael said. 'Our sponsors insisted. They just want a few photos, that's all.'

Danny removed his glasses and ran a hand through his hair.

'Quick!' hissed Maxine's mum. 'Tidy yourself up, girl! You're a mess! You want to look good in the papers, don't you?'

The photographers surrounded them, and Michael was just starting to tell the reporters about Camp Gold International when there was a sudden commotion in the crowd that had gathered, and Maxine heard a high-pitched voice calling out: 'Danny! Danny, darling, where are you? Let me through!'

The crowd parted and Maxine saw a slim, very glamorous young woman teetering towards them on a pair of the highest heels she had ever seen, along with a very short dress that revealed incredibly long legs. She was dragging an enormous leopardskin suitcase behind her and had another huge bag slung over her shoulders. All the press photographers turned round and began snapping away enthusiastically.

'Hi, honey,' said Danny, going to meet her. He

was very close to Maxine and, as he bent close to the girl, she heard him whisper, 'What are you doing here?'

'I'm coming with you,' she replied out of the corner of her mouth, all the time smiling for the cameras. 'What are you waiting for? Give me a kiss.'

Danny kissed her on the cheek and there was another rattle of camera shutters. 'I don't believe it,' said Michael as the photographers moved off. 'They were supposed to interview me about Camp Gold International and I hardly got to say a word. What's going on, Danny?'

'This is Courtney, everyone,' Danny said, a little sheepishly. 'She's my . . . er . . . my new girlfriend. I met her when we were doing a fashion shoot. She's going to be a famous model. And she's coming to Camp Gold. That's OK, isn't it, Michael?'

Maxine could tell that Michael wasn't too

pleased, but he smiled at Courtney. 'Nice to meet you,' he said. 'Any friend of Danny's is very welcome. And now I think we should all check in. Is everybody here?'

'We're missing Jade,' said Isabel. 'She's the last one.'

'There she is,' said John. 'Wave, everyone.'

Jade was a slim, dark-haired girl and she was Maxine's greatest rival, but also a good friend. 'Sorry we're late,' she said as she arrived with her anxious-looking mother. 'We saw all the photographers and decided to stay out of the way.'

'A very good move,' said Isabel, frowning slightly as she looked over to where Courtney was having an argument with the woman on the check-in desk. 'Say your goodbyes, everyone, and let's get on the plane.'

'Have a wonderful time,' said Maxine's mum. 'You've earned it, love. I know it hasn't been easy, but you've done really well. Go on, off you go, before I start crying.'

'*I* won't cry,' said Joshua, giving Maxine a wet kiss on the cheek. 'Make sure you win everything! And look! I bought you this.' He handed Maxine a small bracelet of glittery beads. 'I saved up my pocket money so I could get it for you. It's for luck,' he explained.

'Thanks, Joshua. It's beautiful,' said Maxine, smiling down at her brother and fastening the bracelet on her wrist.

'Wear it for every race,' Joshua called after her as she headed after the others. 'Promise!'

'I promise,' Maxine replied, turning to wave a final goodbye to her family.

Joshua's words were echoing in Maxine's mind as she took her seat on the plane. She had the window seat and Sasha and John were beside her. She looked at the bracelet on her wrist and smiled. Joshua still thought she could win every race, but Maxine knew that now she was going to be training and competing with the best young athletes from all over the world, it wasn't going to be easy.

'I do not know why Danny has brought that silly woman,' Sasha said as they heard Courtney's voice raised again from the back of the plane, complaining about her seat.

'Well, she isn't bad-looking,' said John sheepishly.

'You think she is beautiful?' asked Sasha, turning to look at him. The tips of his ears had gone slightly pink.

'Ooh . . . John's discovered girls,' Maxine giggled, joining in with the teasing.

John went even redder. 'Um . . . well, I don't know,' he muttered. 'Anyway, I guess Danny must like her.'

'Well, then, Danny is a fool.'

Maxine laughed. Sasha had very strong opinions about most things and she always let everyone know what she thought. Her Russian accent always became much stronger when she was angry or excited.

'Danny is a great runner,' Sasha declared. 'How can this woman run in those shoes?'

'I shouldn't think she does,' replied Maxine, giggling again. 'Hey, this is it. We're going to take off.'

The three friends settled back into their seats as the engines roared and the plane accelerated down the runway before rising smoothly into the air. Maxine looked out of the window and saw the familiar landmarks of the city spread out below her: the river, the parks, the football stadiums and houses and streets. There was the running track where she'd been training all year, three or four times a week. Her mum was right. It had been hard sometimes to keep going, especially that time when she had got into serious trouble at school . . .

There had been that awful meeting in the head's office. Mrs Grahame had asked to see Maxine's mum and dad, and Miss Wilson, the PE teacher, had been there too, with Mr Grover, Maxine's class teacher. 'It can't go on, you know, Maxine,' Mrs Grahame had said. 'Your last four pieces of homework have been rushed and your teachers have noticed that your attention has become worse since you started training. It's simply not good enough.'

Maxine had blurted out, 'I know – it's just that there is so much preparation to do for running and I'm always worried about being late for training sessions . . .'

'We're all very proud of your achievements in athletics,' Miss Wilson had interrupted. 'But your education is very important too, more than you realize. You have to focus on your schoolwork too.'

'Maxine will make sure it doesn't happen again,' her dad had said grimly. 'Thank you, Mrs Grahame.'

The row after the meeting had been even worse than the meeting itself. Maxine's dad had been furious. 'You told me you were keeping on top of your schoolwork,' he said. 'You know what'll have to happen, Maxine. You'll have to give up netball, and you'll have to stop going out with your friends at the weekends. Your education must come first. Unless you want to give up running, that is?'

Maxine had shaken her head miserably, knowing that her dad was right. She hated being in trouble at school and she couldn't bear to think of giving up running, so she had started to say no to her friends.

It had been hard at first, and some people who she had thought were friends hadn't wanted to see her any more, but quite a few of the others had started hanging out at the track while she was training. Life wasn't so bad, after all – and, slowly, her schoolwork had begun to improve. But even on the running track things had not exactly gone smoothly.

She had won several races during the year, so Joshua had been pleased, and in two of them she had been running against Jade. She glanced across the aisle now, to where her rival and friend was sitting. Jade smiled at her and then looked down at the magazine she was reading. Jade could afford to smile, thought Maxine ruefully. She had been running faster and faster all year, and now her personal best was almost identical to Maxine's. Despite all her hard work in training, Maxine's times had hardly improved at all for months now.

Beside her, John and Sasha were discussing John's trip back to the United States to visit his grandparents. Maxine joined in with a question, and soon the friends were all laughing together as they remembered the events at last year's Camp Gold.

'Now listen,' said John, lowering his voice. 'Michael and Isabel are being very serious about all this as usual. But we won't let them stop us having a bit of fun too, right?'

Maxine smiled, and suddenly felt very glad she was here. John could be counted on to make sure they did have fun – although she couldn't help recalling Michael's stern warnings when they had stepped out of line the year before. They would have to be very careful not to do anything stupid.

They were flying over high mountains now, and very soon the plane was coming down over a brilliant blue sea. 'There!' exclaimed Sasha, leaning across Maxine to look out of the window as the plane banked into a turn, and they saw the city laid out below them in the dazzling Mediterranean sun. 'There's Barcelona! Where's Camp Gold, Michael?' she called back down the plane.'

'It's up in the hills,' Michael called back. 'You can't see it from here. I think you're all going to be surprised.'

'Why?' asked Maxine, but he didn't answer.

Finally, the plane landed and taxied to a stop. When the plane doors opened, a wave of warm Spanish air wafted in and Maxine felt certain that Camp Gold International was going to be the most amazing thing she had ever done.

CHAPTER TWO

Courtney's two enormous leopardskin suitcases
were already circling on the carousel when
the students arrived to collect their own bags.
Danny grunted as he heaved the first one onto
a trolley.

'Be careful, Danny,' said John mischievously.
'Maybe you should let Courtney do it. You
might pick up another injury!'

Danny laughed. 'I don't know what she's got

in these cases,' he grumbled, with a glance over to where Courtney was standing, inspecting her carefully painted fingernails, 'but it weighs a ton.'

'See you on the bus,' said Maxine, making a grab for her bag as it came past.

'I'm afraid not,' Danny replied. 'I'm hiring a car. Courtney's not that keen on buses.'

'I bet she's not,' said Jade, watching as Danny and Courtney disappeared from sight.

'Right then,' said Michael, looking around at the assembled students. 'Have you all got your bags? Let's go to Camp Gold International. You should be impressed.'

As they walked through the bustling airport Maxine heard the sound of Spanish voices all around her. The air smelled different. She was in a foreign country for the first time in her life!

'You have to speak two languages in Barcelona,' John said knowledgeably. He had been here before. 'This is Catalonia, so the main language is Catalan, but everyone speaks Spanish too.'

'I do not think Courtney speaks either of those languages,' said Sasha.

They all looked over to the car-hire stand, where Courtney was shouting at the woman behind the desk – in English: 'I don't care if it's booked out to someone else. That's the car we want. Do you know who you're talking to? This is Danny Crowe.'

Danny looked very embarrassed. He put a hand on Courtney's arm, but she shrugged it off angrily and carried on shouting.

'She is a total nightmare,' said Sasha as they emerged from the air-conditioned airport and the dusty heat of the Spanish afternoon hit them.

'Forget about her,' John said, climbing aboard the bus. They settled into their seats. 'Michael seems to think that Camp Gold International is going to be a big surprise, but I can't imagine

how it can possibly be better than last year's.
I can't wait to see it. Do any of you know
anything?'

They all shook their heads.

'I wonder how far it is from the sea,' Maxine
said, and they all began talking about the beach
party that had nearly resulted in them being
thrown out of Camp Gold the year before.

'You are wrong about the sea,' Sasha said.
'I think we are going inland.'

The bus had been travelling through the
suburbs, past blocks of flats and industrial
buildings, but now it had turned off the main
road onto a smaller one and was starting to climb
into scrub-covered hills. Fifteen minutes later
Michael stood up at the front of the bus. 'There
you are,' he said, bending slightly and pointing
through the window. 'Camp Gold International!'

All along the bus the students craned their
necks to see what Michael was pointing at.

'No!' said Maxine. 'It can't be.' She was looking across the rocky landscape towards a line of craggy cliffs topped with trees and there, rising above everything, were the sheer walls of a castle. From a flagpole on top of a grim-looking tower, the distinctive Camp Gold flag was flying.

'Where's the running track?' asked John. 'There's nowhere flat around here. Where are we going to train?'

'Just wait,' said Michael, smiling as the bus began to climb steadily through pine woods. Eventually it emerged from the woods into a broad valley with low hills on either side and they finally saw Camp Gold International in all its glory. The ancient walls of the remains of the castle were dwarfed by a complex of modern buildings set at the back of an expanse of parkland. The grass looked impossibly green against the backdrop of brown hills. Away beyond the gleaming new buildings Maxine saw the tower of the castle.

'There is just a bit of the old castle left,' Isabel told them as they stood in front of the sliding glass doors at the entrance to the main building. 'It was mostly ruined, but they managed to save a few rooms. Some of you girls will be staying up there. Maxine, Sasha, Jade, we've put you three in the tower. I think you'll enjoy it. But don't try climbing out of the windows!'

Maxine felt herself flushing, and she saw that Sasha was looking embarrassed too. The year before, they had climbed out of their windows to go to a beach party. It looked like they wouldn't be able to do that again.

'Off you go, then,' said Isabel, with the hint of a smile. 'Collect your luggage and you'll find your keys inside.'

'What are we waiting for?' said Maxine. 'Let's go!'

The three girls seized their bags and dashed in through the glass doors. Most of the keys on the table were plastic smart cards, but there were also several heavy metal keys with brass tags attached to them. A girl about their own age with large eyes, very black hair and a pale face told them where to go. 'Through the doors and along the . . . I do not know the word . . . then up the stairs.'

'Are you Spanish?' asked John, coming up behind them.

'No. I am Catalan!' The girl's eyes flashed at them. 'My name is Rosalita. I am working here for vacation. I live in town.' She pointed towards the valley beyond the green playing fields of Camp Gold International.

'Your English is terrific,' John said with a smile, and the girl blushed. 'It's called a corridor.'

'Corridor,' she repeated carefully, smiling at John. 'Thank you.'

'We're going to find our rooms,' Maxine told John, who was still gazing into Rosalita's eyes. 'We'll meet back here, OK?'

'I think he likes her,' Sasha giggled as they walked down the long corridor.

'I kind of liked her too,' Maxine replied. 'Look, this is where the old part begins.'

More sliding glass doors opened ahead of them, and they saw a stone wall blocking their way. To their right a flight of stairs spiralled upwards. Lights were embedded in the stone steps and shone from the walls as they climbed. They came to a landing and saw the doors of three rooms. 'We have to go higher,' Sasha said, looking at the numbers on the doors and indicating an archway that led to more stairs. 'We must be on the top floor.'

As they were crossing the landing one of the doors opened and a tall, slender black girl appeared and smiled shyly at them before moving off down the stairs. They climbed up past two more landings and finally came to their own rooms. 'It's like our own private place,' Jade said. 'But I hope it won't be too uncomfortable. It's really old.'

Maxine was already fitting her key into the ancient lock. The door opened and she gasped in astonishment. The walls of the room were the original stone walls of the castle, but the floor was of polished wood and the furniture was new and elegant. The door to the bathroom was open and she could see a floor of smooth grey stone and a gleaming shower. But the best thing of all was the window. There was a recessed archway at the far side of the room with a broad stone windowsill that was big enough to sit on. The tall window looked out over a dizzying view of hills and the plain below, all shimmering in a heat haze.

'Awesome,' breathed Maxine, and she heard

similar exclamations of amazement from the other rooms. She ran through to join Sasha and saw that her friend's window looked out along the crest of the tree-lined ridge, though Sasha herself was over at the other side checking out the shower facilities. They both went into Jade's room and found her sitting on her windowsill, her knees drawn up under her chin. Her view was like Sasha's but in the opposite direction.

'It's like being on top of the world,' she said. 'I could sit here for ever.'

'No, you couldn't,' said Maxine, laughing. 'We can't be late for Michael's welcome speech.'

They all locked their doors and ran down the three flights of spiral stairs. 'I think Isabel wanted us up here so we could get fit,' Sasha said when they arrived at the bottom.

'I'm not so sure,' said Maxine. 'I think she meant what she said about us not climbing out of windows. She's making sure we can't do that again.'

'We would need a very long rope, I think,' said Sasha, and for a moment Maxine thought she was serious. The previous year they had all climbed out of their windows in the middle of the night with the help of Sasha's vaulting pole. Then Sasha burst out laughing, her green eyes glittering, and they were all laughing with her as they entered the main building and saw the line of students waiting to enter the room where the meeting was taking place.

John joined them as they went through a door and found themselves at the back of a lecture hall with seats that sloped down towards a kind of stage at the bottom. Michael was waiting there with a large screen behind him and a laptop computer on the desk in front. Maxine looked around curiously and saw an astonishing collection of faces from every corner of the world. Two rows behind them she saw the girl they'd met earlier on the landing. She waved and the girl waved back. Maxine could see that she looked very nervous and felt a pang of sympathy as Michael began to speak.

'As you know,' he began, 'we founded Camp Gold to develop undiscovered talent. Now, of course, all of you have been discovered! By us! But we want to show the whole world what Camp Gold can do, and our sponsors, Galactic Sportswear, have paid for you all to come and be together for three weeks. We hope that you can learn from each other and that the competition will inspire you all to even more success. Your coaches will give you further information when you start training tomorrow. Remember, though, you have been given an amazing opportunity – don't waste it. I expect to see hard work and discipline. Messing around will not be tolerated.'

There was silence for a moment, then Michael

smiled broadly and all traces of his previous seriousness disappeared. 'Right, that's the serious bit over; now you have a couple of hours to explore this place before we eat. It's a fabulous setting, and you'll be pleased to know that you'll be allowed to use the marked trails in the countryside near the camp in your free time, as long as you're in a group and you let us know where you're going. But for now, there's plenty to see inside Camp Gold. Enjoy yourselves, and I'll see you all later.'

'All right,' said John when they were outside. 'I think the first thing we should do is find the basketball court.'

'Right,' agreed Maxine. 'There must be one. Michael would have made sure of that.'

Maxine, John and Sasha were all fanatical basketball players and they knew that both Michael and Danny Crowe loved the game. They had enjoyed some long, close-fought pick-up matches the year before, and they were all eager to resume them.

They found the basketball court on the top of the cliff behind an Astroturf football pitch. It was surrounded on three sides by ancient pine trees. On the fourth side, only a high wire fence separated the court from the vertical drop a few metres beyond it. A ball was lying on the ground, almost as if it was waiting for them, and John was just picking it up when they all heard the sound of voices approaching. Michael and Danny were there, and so were a group of about ten young athletes.

'I knew we'd find you here,' Danny said. 'We thought we'd better round up a team to help us to take you on.'

'You can't have all of them,' exclaimed Maxine, noticing the tall black girl with the shy smile hovering at the back of the group.

'We'll let you have a few,' Michael said. 'But

we want to keep Hiari and Cheng. And I think we'll have Hui Zhong, Ravul and Diane too,' he said, indicating the five players standing closest to him. 'Right. Shall we start? May the best team win!'

The game was fast and furious. Michael and Danny had selected their team carefully and Maxine wondered how Michael had managed it. The tall black girl was called Hiari, and she was simply amazing. She could leap like a wild deer and Maxine wondered if maybe she was a high-jumper, but she never had time to ask her as she slammed in basket after basket and Michael grinned with wicked satisfaction.

Finally they stopped for a break. 'At last, we're beating you,' Danny Crowe said.

'It's not fair,' replied Maxine. 'I bet you went through everyone's records and found out who was good at basketball,' she added, looking challengingly at Michael.

He shrugged. 'I just asked if anyone fancied a game,' he said, his eyes twinkling with amusement. 'Can I help it if Hiari happens to be in her national junior team?'

'I knew it,' said John, shaking his head. 'Well, we'll just have to improve, that's all. Come on, guys, we can beat a couple of old men, even if they do have help.'

'Who are you calling old?' retorted Danny. 'I'm the world four-hundred–metres champion. Give me that ball.'

But before he could restart the game they all heard a familiar shrill voice: 'Danny, where are you?' and Courtney appeared on the far side of the court. She had changed into a pair of pink leggings and a green strapless top. She took off her dark glasses and peered at the group on the basketball court. 'What are you doing, Danny?' she demanded. 'We're going out, remember. It's Saturday night! Go and get the car.'

'Sorry, guys,' Danny said with a shrug as he turned to face them. 'I guess I have to go. You can beat them without me, right, Michael? And I have to think about my hamstring. See you later!'

He picked up his top and jogged off to join Courtney. Michael shook his head as he watched him go. Then he turned back and saw them all watching him. He smiled, but not before Maxine had observed an odd expression on his face, half irritation, half-concern.

'Danny's right,' Michael said cheerfully to his team. 'We don't need him, do we, guys?' He flung the ball to Hiari, and the game resumed.

Half an hour later they were still playing when they saw an enormous black four-wheel-drive car purr away down the drive. A hand emerged from the driver's window and waved to them. Danny, heading out with Courtney.

'This is very bad,' said Sasha darkly when the game finally broke up a few minutes later and the friends were walking back to their rooms. 'We must save Danny from this terrible woman.'

CHAPTER THREE

The next morning Maxine woke early, jumped out of bed and ran to the window. It wasn't a dream. She really was sleeping in a room high up in the tower of an ancient Spanish castle and the countryside already looked hot under a glaring blue sky.

She called for Sasha and Jade and the three girls descended the spiral staircase together. When they passed Hiari's door Maxine paused.

'Let's see if she wants to have breakfast with us,' she said.

Hiari looked puzzled for a moment when she opened the door, then her face was lit by a smile. 'Hi,' she said. 'Do you want to play basketball?'

'Not right now,' Maxine replied. 'Come down to breakfast. We want to know how you got so good at it.'

The restaurant was on the ground floor of the part of the castle that had been restored. There were plenty of empty tables inside because everyone seemed to be eating on the terrace, which looked out over the edge of the cliff. The students could choose from a bewildering variety of breakfast food, but Maxine's eyes were drawn to some long thin doughnuts on the counter. 'Wow!' she exclaimed. 'What are they?'

'Churros,' said Rosalita, the girl they had spoken to the day before, who was now serving the breakfasts. 'They are like doughnuts. You eat them with hot chocolate, see?' She showed them the bowl of dark, thick-looking chocolate she was about to give to the boy ahead of them in the queue.

'Mmmm,' said Maxine. 'I'll have some of that, please.'

'Make the most of it,' said Michael Gladstone, joining the queue behind them, Isabel beside him. 'We're only serving them today to give you a little taste of Spain.'

'They're not exactly healthy eating,' laughed Isabel. 'But don't worry. You'll still have excellent breakfasts. This is Camp Gold International, after all.'

'I see you've made friends with my new basketball signing,' Michael said. 'Make sure you don't get her into trouble.'

'What did he mean by that?' asked Hiari when they were settled at a table. Maxine couldn't answer because her mouth was full of churros and chocolate. The chocolate was deliciously rich and sticky.

'He was teasing us,' said Sasha. 'We had some fun at Camp Gold last year, that's all. We went to a party on the beach in the middle of the night and Michael caught us.'

'But he let us off in the end,' said John, who had joined them at the table. 'He told us himself that he wasn't always perfect when he was younger.'

'I think Isabel reckons he is perfect now,' said Sasha, and they all looked over at the table in the corner where Isabel was gazing into Michael's eyes and holding his hand.

'Well, they have just got married,' said Maxine, who was a little worried by how much John seemed to have forgotten about the year before. They had actually been in serious trouble, but John made it sound like a joke. It hadn't been. 'Hey, Hiari,' she said, changing the subject, 'how did you learn to play basketball like that?'

'At my school,' said Hiari. 'I am very lucky. I was top of my class in my local village school and I was sent to a big school in the city.'

'How old were you?' asked Maxine, suddenly thinking of her own family back home.

'I was ten years old,' Hiari said. 'I cried at first, but it was a very good school and I wanted to learn about everything. And I learned to play basketball too.'

'What about your village?' asked John. 'What was that like?'

'Very small,' Hiari said. 'My school was four miles away from my home. I ran there every morning, and back again every night. I was the fastest runner in the village.'

'And you still like running, after all that?' asked Maxine, astonished.

'I love it,' said Hiari. 'I love it even more than basketball. Even more than these!' She took a large bite of churro, and chocolate dribbled down her chin.

Maxine suddenly realized that she was sweating. They had been sitting in the shade, but as they'd been talking the sun had found them and was beating down on the stones of the terrace all around them. 'I hope it's not going to be this hot all the time,' she said.

Hiari laughed. 'This isn't hot,' she said. 'Where I come from it is far hotter than this. The African sun is very strong.'

'Oh.' It occurred to Maxine that quite a few of the other athletes who were here would be far more accustomed to the heat than she was. 'So what's your event?' she asked Hiari.

'We thought you might be a high-jumper,' Sasha said.

'Or even a pole-vaulter like Sasha,' said John.

'No,' said Hiari, shaking her head. 'I run eight hundred metres.'

Jade and Maxine exchanged glances. 'The same as us,' said Jade. 'What's your personal best?'

Hiari told them, and for a moment neither girl could speak. Hiari's personal best was eight-tenths of a second faster than their own. 'How about you?' she asked them. But before they could reply they were interrupted.

'Can I sit here?' asked Courtney brightly, then pulled up an extra chair and sat down without waiting for a reply. Her hair was up and a pair of dark glasses covered half her face. She was wearing a pair of very short shorts and a skimpy top.

'I hope you did not forget to put on sun block,' Sasha said as Courtney arranged her long brown legs to achieve maximum exposure to the sun. As before, Danny's girlfriend was wearing very high heels and she pointed her toes as she stretched out.

Courtney laughed, a high-pitched tinkling

laugh. 'You are funny,' she said. 'As if I would burn myself! I have to look just right all the time, you know. It's my job to look good.'

Maxine thought Courtney looked ridiculous, but she didn't say so. Danny's girlfriend had a plate of sliced-up fruit and berries for her breakfast, with a few nuts and seeds mixed in, but Maxine noticed her looking enviously at the churros.

'So tell me,' said Courtney as she nibbled at her meagre breakfast. 'What do you all do? I bet you're all terribly sporty.'

'Well, this *is* an athletics camp,' John said with a grin, 'so I guess it would be kind of strange if we weren't. We're all runners except for Sasha here. She's a pole-vaulter.'

'Oh,' said Courtney, looking surprised. 'I thought that was a kind of dancing.'

They all burst out laughing, but they stopped when they saw Courtney looking offended.

'You jump over a very high bar and you use a pole to help you,' Sasha explained. Maxine could see that she was finding it hard to keep a straight face.

'I don't know how you can do it,' Courtney said. 'Running around outside all day in this heat. It's much nicer in the gym. But I was wondering, do you need a lot of special equipment for what you do?'

'Special equipment?' said Maxine. 'What kind of equipment?'

'There's Sasha's pole,' said Jade. 'That's equipment for sure.'

'Well, you know, your shoes and . . . things . . . Your shoes must be special ones, I suppose. They must cost lots of money.'

'You mean, like these?' said Maxine with a laugh, lifting one foot and putting it on the edge of the table. She was wearing her oldest, most comfortable trainers. The laces were frayed and bits had fallen off them.

Courtney gave a little squeal and stood up, waving Maxine's foot away. 'That's disgusting! Oh, look, there's Danny. He's going somewhere. Danny, sweetie, I'm coming! Wait for me!' She stood up and teetered off on her heels without another glance at the friends around the table.

'How can Danny stand it?' whispered Jade, looking around the table in bewilderment. 'I know I couldn't.'

'Was she asking us those questions seriously, or was she trying to wind us up?' asked John. 'She's going out with an Olympic champion. She must know *something* about sport.'

'It doesn't look like it,' said Jade. 'Let's talk about something else. Do you think we'll be allowed to explore the countryside? Will we have days out?'

They chatted on for nearly half an hour before Jade suddenly looked at her watch. 'Come on, we should get moving. Training starts soon. We don't want to be late.'

They all stood up, but Sasha bent down to look on the floor under the table. She straightened, scratching her head. 'I don't understand it,' she said. 'My key was right here, I'm sure it was.'

They all joined in with the search. 'I suppose it could have fallen on the floor and someone might have accidentally kicked it away,' said John, when they couldn't find it near the table. They widened the search to the other nearby tables, but couldn't find the key anywhere.

'What's the problem?' asked Michael when they asked if they could look behind the table where he was sitting with Isabel.

'I have lost my key,' said Sasha. 'What am I going to do? How can I have done something so stupid?'

'Hey,' said Isabel sympathetically. 'Don't worry

about it, Sasha. I lose my keys all the time. I'm sure the janitor will let you in. He has an office just by the main entrance. Your key will turn up, I bet.'

'I know where the janitor is,' said John. 'Come on, I'll show you.'

'We'll all go,' said Maxine.

It was a long walk through the modern part of Camp Gold to the main entrance.

'So soon?' said the janitor, shaking his head. 'You have only just arrived. Wait, I will fetch key.' He was a plump, elderly Spanish man with thick, black hair and a rash of blue stubble on his pale cheeks. His name was Juan. He retrieved a key from a cupboard at the back of his office and led the way back along the corridor and up the stairs into the tower. He grumbled quietly as he climbed the stone spirals and stopped at each landing to regain his breath.

Finally they emerged onto the top landing.

The janitor stopped. Sasha's door was wide open. He looked at the number on the key, then back at the door.

'Your key is not lost,' he said finally. 'There it is, look. You left it in your door.'

They crossed the landing and looked into the room. Sasha's hands went up to her face and she gasped. 'I don't understand,' she said. 'Look at this!'

The room was a mess. The bedclothes lay on the floor. All Sasha's things had been pulled from the drawers and tossed around everywhere. 'This is very bad way to look after your room,' said the janitor, frowning. 'You must keep it tidy or the cleaners cannot clean. And you should remember to lock the door. I do not wish to keep climbing all these stairs. There are many rooms in the new building and I told them they should have put you there, but they would not listen.'

He was still grumbling to himself – now in Spanish, or Catalan – as he went off down the stairs.

'I don't understand it,' said Sasha again. 'I locked my door. I know I did. You all saw me.'

'Someone must have taken your key and done this,' Maxine said. 'But it doesn't make any sense. You haven't upset anyone, have you? Not like last year.'

When they had all been together the year before they had been drawn into a silly feud with another group of students, but they had all become friends eventually. This was exactly the kind of trick that they might have played on each other, though.

'Maybe it was one of the basketball players,' Maxine suggested weakly. 'They're the only people we've met so far. Maybe you pushed one of them or something?'

It was a limp explanation, but Sasha

considered it seriously for a moment before shaking her head. 'No. Definitely not. It was a very fun game.'

'Think about it the other way,' said Jade suddenly. 'Who had a chance to steal your key? We went straight down to breakfast, remember? We went to the counter, then we sat at our table. You put your key on your tray. I remember seeing it.'

'So it could only have been the girl who was serving,' said Maxine, thinking back, 'or Michael or Isabel, but that's ridiculous. Or the boy in front of us in the queue . . .?'

'Or Courtney!' said Sasha. 'I'm sure I still had the key when we went outside, so it must have been her. I told you she was very strange.'

'That's crazy,' said Jade. 'I know she's annoying, but why would she do a thing like this?'

'I don't know,' said Maxine grimly. 'But someone did.'

CHAPTER FOUR

Maxine and Jade helped Sasha to tidy her room. 'Is anything missing?' asked Maxine.

Sasha shook her head, her face still flushed with anger. 'Nothing. It is crazy. Why would she do this?'

'If it was her,' said Maxine doubtfully. The girls collected their things and went back down to meet John. They told him what had happened.

'We think it might have been Courtney,' said Jade.

'No way,' said John. 'Why would an adult pull a prank like this? And I doubt if she could have climbed the stairs in those shoes.'

'I bet she's only about twenty,' replied Jade. 'My sister's older than that and she's always messing around.'

'We'd better keep our eyes open,' Maxine said as they walked down the path leading to the track. Her footsteps slowed as they left the shade of the pine trees behind. 'I can't believe we're going to be training when it's this hot.'

'It gets hotter,' John said. 'That's why we had breakfast so early. I checked the schedule. We only do an hour now and then more early tomorrow morning.'

'I don't think I can do five minutes,' said Maxine.

'Of course you can,' Sasha told her. 'We all can. This will be very hard, but we will succeed.'

Maxine laughed. Sasha was amazing. She couldn't imagine anything that would stop the passionate Russian girl. They had arrived at the track and Maxine suddenly glimpsed a familiar face amid the small crowd that had gathered in the sparse shade of a group of pine trees. 'Kath!' she exclaimed. 'Is that you?'

A thin, muscular, very bronzed woman with short, streaked blonde hair detached herself from the group and came to meet them. Kath had been Maxine and Jade's running coach at Camp Gold the previous year, but neither of them had seen her since the National Indoor Championships several months ago.

'Wow!' said Kath, beaming. 'Just look at you all! It's so great to see you.'

'You weren't on the plane,' said Jade. 'We thought you wouldn't be here.'

'Someone has to get all this ready for you guys,' Kath told them, with a wide gesture of her arms. 'I've been back home in Oz for a while, but when Michael asked me if I wanted to come, well, I jumped at it. I'm excited to be your chief coach! Which reminds me – I need to make an announcement to everyone.' She gathered all the athletes together. 'We'll just be doing some light training this morning,' she told them. 'Think of it as a chance for us all to get to know each other, and for some of you it'll be a chance to get used to the climate.'

Maxine looked around at the expectant faces and heard a low buzz of chatter – in about twenty different languages!

Kath held up a hand for quiet. 'I've got some very exciting news for you. At the end of your three weeks here, you'll be competing in a major exhibition event. Guess where?'

'Here?' suggested Maxine.

'Not far from here. In the Olympic Stadium in Barcelona.'

There was another burst of excited conversation. 'That's not all,' Kath went on. 'You'll be running at the same event as the world's top performers. Every adult event will be followed by a junior event featuring Camp Gold athletes. That's you!'

'You mean, there'll be an eight hundred metres with people like . . . like Kerry Jones?' Jade asked, mentioning the current fastest 800-metre runner in the world. 'And then . . . us?'

'You've got the idea,' replied Kath. 'There should be a crowd of about fifty thousand people watching you too.'

Maxine hoped that her face didn't show the terror she suddenly felt. Her heart was beating fast and the sweat on her face had turned cold. Running in front of fifty thousand spectators was a seriously scary prospect and she wasn't sure she could do it.

Kath was looking at them all with an amused expression. 'You look like frightened rabbits,' she said. 'But there's no need for you to worry. By the time you've had three weeks with the finest coaches in the world, you'll be ready for anything. Plus there's an extra incentive for all of you. The winners of every event will get the chance to carry the Olympic torch through their home town next year. How does that sound?'

It sounded wonderful to Maxine, but only one 800-metre runner could win, and as she began the training session it didn't seem that it was likely to be her. The hot sun beat down on the athletes as they all ran two laps of the track at a gentle jog before separating off into their various groups. For the first time Maxine saw all the distance runners together. She looked furtively around as they began a series of stretches. She knew about Hiari and Jade, but there wasn't a single athlete there who didn't look focused and strong. She watched the muscles rippling in the legs of Hui Zhong, the compact Chinese girl who had played basketball the night before. She looked very tough, and then there was Estrella, a tall, dark-skinned girl from Argentina—

'Hey, come on, Maxine! Concentrate!' Kath's voice cut into her reverie and she realized that they had all moved on to a different exercise. She was going to have to do better than this.

Kath led them onto a wide grassy playing field, which was situated beside the track. 'We're going to work on tempo,' she said. 'I'm going to split you into two groups of eight and I'd like each group to run a random course on the field and arrive back here in exactly forty-five seconds. You can take it as fast or as slow as you like. Hiari, you lead Team One. Hui Zhong, you take Team Two.'

Maxine was in Team Two. Kath blew her whistle, stopwatch in hand, and the two teams set off. Hui Zhong set a fast pace as she led them out around the field, and Maxine soon found herself at the back of the line of runners. She saw that Hiari's group had already started heading back towards Kath, but Hui Zhong showed no sign of turning yet. Maxine realized guiltily that she hadn't even been trying to keep track of the time.

Then the leader suddenly turned for home and increased the pace. 'She got it wrong,' grunted Jade, dropping back beside Maxine. 'But she can certainly sprint.'

Maxine had no breath to reply. When they reached Kath her legs were burning and the sweat was soaking her running vest. 'Fifty-three seconds,' Kath said. 'Not bad, but Team One were spot on. Well done, Hiari! The aim is to run at a constant pace, Hui Zhong – not to speed up at the end, OK?'

The Chinese girl nodded. 'We'll have thirty seconds' rest,' Kath told them, 'then we'll do it again with different leaders.'

Kath had been clever, thought Maxine, as they set off again with a powerfully built Canadian girl named Jerry in the lead; this was a very good way of getting to know each other. Hui Zhong had been impulsive and had relied on her sprinting ability to fix things when they went wrong. Jerry was far more cautious, moving at a gentle jog and keeping a close eye on the other team. They arrived back only two seconds over time, and then it was Jade's turn to lead.

Maxine wasn't surprised when Jade led them back perfectly on time. Sometimes she thought that Jade must have a clock hard-wired into her brain, the way she could run laps in a set time.

But now it was her own turn, and she was feeling tired. She took a drink from her water-bottle and forced herself to concentrate. If she led them at the same pace as Jerry had done, and ran roughly the same route, then it should be OK. But as she reached the point where she felt she should turn for home she knew that she had been running too slowly. It was the heat. She speeded up, but her legs seemed to be slow in obeying her brain, and they were five seconds late arriving back.

'Drink more water, Maxine,' Kath said. 'All of you need to make sure you take on enough fluids. It's going to take you a while to acclimatize, but believe me, you will. We'll do some interval training on the track and then we'll be finished for this morning.'

'I don't know if I can do this,' Maxine whispered to Jade as they walked onto the track. 'It's hotter than an oven out here.'

'No, it's not,' Jade replied. 'Hey, listen, if you think about it, we're representing our country here. Let's show them we can handle it.'

'OK, guys,' said Kath. 'If you're all ready you're going to do four two-hundred-metre sprints with two hundred metres recovery in between each one. Run the sprints as fast as you can. There are cones marking the changes. Jog the first two hundred. Go!'

Maxine jogged along beside Jade, watching the first of the cones coming ever closer. As they reached it, Kath sent out a blast on her whistle and suddenly they were all running flat out. Maxine pushed herself as hard as she could, but at the end of the sprint she was several metres behind the pack and there was nothing she could do about it.

She caught them up as they jogged through the recovery phase, but when the whistle blew they streaked away from her again. At the end of the session she eyed the others gloomily as she warmed down with Jade.

'Don't worry about it,' Jade said, seeing the expression on her face. 'You're one of the best runners I've ever seen. You're a bit tired, that's all.'

'Thanks. Maybe you're right. Only . . .'

'What?'

'Your times keep getting better, right? All year they've been improving, but mine have just stayed the same. It feels like it did out there on the track. Everyone else is running away from me.'

'I don't think so,' Jade said briskly. 'Come on, Kath wants us.'

'Now, listen,' Kath said when all the athletes were together. 'There's one more thing I have to tell you, but I have to ask you all to keep this dead secret. You all know that Camp Gold International is sponsored by Galactic Sportswear?' They could hardly help knowing, thought Maxine; they were all wearing training gear with the company's logo splashed across the front. 'Well, Galactic have asked us to trial a revolutionary new running shoe,' Kath continued. 'They say it could improve times significantly. If they're right then we might see a good many world records broken next year, and you guys will be the first athletes to try these shoes.'

'Maybe we'll break records,' said John. 'Can these shoes knock ten seconds off my time?'

Kath laughed. 'Only hard work will do that, John.'

'Do we get to keep the shoes?' asked Jade.

Kath smiled and shook her head. 'This really is top secret,' she said. 'The shoes are prototypes. They're called Meganova, and they'll be going back to the factory. You mustn't tell anyone about this, not even your families. Galactic have competitors who would love to get their hands on these shoes. OK, that's it, everyone. See you back here bright and early tomorrow morning.' Just at that moment, her phone rang. She took it out, looked at the screen and frowned. 'Michael wants everyone back at lecture theatre,' she said. 'I don't know what's going on, but it sounds urgent.'

There were groans from the tired athletes. 'Can't we take a shower first?' asked John.

For an answer Kath showed him the screen of her phone. The word NOW was written in capital letters, followed by a string of exclamation marks.

They hurried back to the central building and filed into the lecture theatre. Most people were still finding their seats when Michael stormed into the room and stood impatiently in front of them.

'We've had a break-in,' he said. 'In my office. It's too soon to say what's been taken, but the whole place has been turned upside down. If this is some stupid prank, then whoever did it will discover that there's no place for that kind of thing here. And when we find the people responsible I promise you that they'll be on the first plane home. They're finished at Camp Gold!'

CHAPTER FIVE

The following day the athletes assembled at the track at six-thirty in the morning. It had been a struggle to wake so early, but Maxine was glad now that she had. It was warm, but there was a freshness in the breeze that trickled down from the hills, and an aromatic scent of pine trees and herbs in the air.

After warming up they set off on a course through the grounds that took them up steep slopes among the trees and onto a flat, grassy area where they went through a series of sprints.

'How are you feeling?' asked Jade as they walked to the next set of exercises.

'Good.' Maxine nodded. She could see Michael in the distance and she pointed him out to her friend. 'Do you think they've found out who broke into Michael's office yet?'

'I don't know. No one's said anything.'

'All right, you two,' called Kath. 'This is a workout, not a walk in the country. We'll take this next slope fast.' She sprinted off up the hill.

Jade pulled a face at Maxine. 'She's in a terrible mood,' she said as they set off in pursuit. 'All the coaches are.'

It was true. There had been a heavy atmosphere in Camp Gold ever since Michael's announcement of the break-in. As Maxine ran up the hill, the soft bed of pine needles crunching gently beneath her feet, she remembered how they had all argued about it the night before as they sat on the terrace while stars winked out in the sky and the lights of houses and villages appeared on the hazy plain below.

'Well, I do not care what all of you think,' Sasha had said. 'I am sure it was Courtney who did it.'

'That's crazy,' said John. 'I don't even think Courtney was here. She keeps dragging Danny away to Barcelona. He never seems to be around and I was looking forward to getting some coaching from him.'

'I wish he would spend more time here too,' Sasha said. 'I like seeing his handsome face around.'

'Courtney seems to think Danny came here just to drive her around in that stupid car,' said Jade. 'You can see Michael is annoyed.'

'Well, Michael has plenty to be annoyed

about,' said John, returning to the subject of the trashed office. 'But it can't have been Courtney. I reckon it has to be someone who's broken in. Just an ordinary burglar.'

'That's not what Michael thinks,' Maxine said. 'You heard him. He thinks it's someone in the camp. He suspects everyone. Even us.'

'No, he doesn't,' said Sasha. 'Why would he?'

'Because he thinks it might be someone playing stupid tricks,' said John gloomily. 'Maxine's right. We weren't exactly the perfect students last year, were we?'

The evening had been spoiled and Maxine had gone to bed early. But now, despite Kath's snappy mood, she found that she was enjoying the early-morning training. She was still feeling good when Kath told them at the end of the session that they would run a timed 800. There were sixteen athletes and they ran in two groups of eight. Maxine watched as Jade pushed herself to the limit to try to keep up with Hiari in the first race, but Hiari seemed to flow effortlessly round the track in a blur of smooth movement and finished two metres ahead of Jade.

'Good work, all of you,' Kath said, looking up from the clipboard where she had noted down their times; she was smiling for the first time that morning. 'Jade, you just ran a PB. Look! Half a second improvement.'

'That's awesome!' exclaimed Maxine.

Jade glanced at her and Maxine hoped her words didn't sound false. She was pleased for Jade, but she was alarmed too. How was she ever going to catch up?

'Next group,' called Kath, and Maxine moved nervously forward to her starting position. She eyed the Chinese girl, Hui Zhong, anxiously. She knew Hui Zhong was fast, but not exactly how fast. She decided she would stick with her, and she stayed two paces behind her, all the way round the first circuit of the track, but she was taken by surprise on the back straight when Jerry, the Canadian girl, powered past both of them.

Hui Zhong sprinted to catch her up, but although Maxine tried to respond she found that she couldn't keep pace with the Chinese girl, and as they raced towards the finish two other runners also passed her. She waited anxiously for Kath to reveal their times. At least if she had run a PB that would be something. But when Kath looked up and caught her eye she knew at once that she hadn't. Kath had all their times logged: personal bests and their times for all their competitions over the past year.

'You're consistent, anyway,' Kath told Maxine. 'Nought point one outside your PB. Jerry, that was a terrific run. Three-tenths faster. Well done!'

'I don't understand it,' Maxine said to Jade as

they walked back after training. 'I don't feel as if I'm doing anything differently, but I just don't get any faster. I must be doing something wrong.'

Jade was sympathetic, but Maxine knew that there wasn't really much she could say. Besides, she was obviously thrilled with her own time. Camp Gold International wasn't turning out the way Maxine had dreamed.

And for the next two days it only got worse . . .

It wasn't that she was running badly exactly, but with each training session that came and went Maxine failed to improve, and she desperately wanted to. She wanted to race against these girls from every part of the world and beat them. She wanted to win, but somehow she had lost that magical ingredient that helped her to do it, and she didn't know how to get it back.

It was their fourth full day at Camp Gold and another training session was almost over. Maxine had pushed herself as hard as she could all morning and now, as Kath told them they were going to run time trials, her legs felt horribly heavy. Suddenly she couldn't face the thought of chasing hopelessly after the other girls yet again.

'I'm sorry, Kath,' she said. 'I'm not feeling well. It's my tummy.'

The others gave her sympathetic looks as she picked up her things and hurried off to the locker room. Once inside she showered quickly and then sat on a bench feeling a little ashamed. It wasn't long before she heard the other athletes returning, and a laughing, chattering throng burst in through the door.

'Are you OK?' asked Hiari, seeing her sitting there.

But before Maxine could answer there was an exclamation from one of the other girls, an American from California with streaked blonde hair who looked to Maxine as if she'd walked straight out of a TV series. Her name was Martha. 'Someone's been going through my bag!' she said. 'Look. My iPod was in the bottom, I know it was, and now it's on the top.'

'No way,' said Jade. 'Why would anyone search your bag and not take your iPod? It doesn't make sense.'

'Well, they did. You should all check your bags.' With that, Martha cast a suspicious glance at Maxine.

Maxine looked away. It was too bad. She had done nothing, but there was no way she could prove it. She felt very relieved when nobody else found anything wrong with their bags.

'I would never know anyway,' said Jade, looking up. 'I just throw everything in.'

'Me too,' agreed Jerry. 'No one's actually stolen anything, have they?' she asked Martha.

'Well, no,' admitted the American girl, 'but—'

'That's OK, then,' Jerry said briskly. 'Things are

bad enough already around here. Let's not make it any worse.'

The next day was a rest day for the young athletes – the coaches wanted to give them a little time off before a mini-competition scheduled for the next day. When they had finished eating breakfast, two buses were waiting to take them into the nearby town. It was only a short drive down from the rocky, tree-covered ridge where the castle stood into the shallow valley lined with fields of well-tended vegetables. When they arrived in the town, they discovered that it was market day.

They walked up a bustling street with honey-coloured buildings on either side of them and narrow alleyways leading off in every direction. They passed a group of men on ladders; they were hanging strings of brightly coloured flags from the guttering and Isabel, who had accompanied them into town with several of the athletics coaches, told them that the town was getting ready for a fiesta.

'Is it today?' asked Hiari. 'This looks like a lot of fun.'

'No, it's on Saturday. And I dare say it will be fun,' replied Isabel, 'but I don't think any of you will be going. It was all I could do to persuade Michael to let you take this little trip, so make sure you don't get lost. This is the marketplace, as you can see. Be back here in an hour. The church clock will strike twelve, and you'll hear it.'

At that moment the harsh clang of the clock rang out above the canvas roofs of the market stalls, striking eleven. The market was busy. Stalls selling bread, cheese and vegetables mingled with others displaying household goods or piles of old metal tools. Maxine soon tired of browsing among the stalls – she really wanted to explore some of the shaded alleyways leading away from the square. 'I'm just going to take a look, OK?' she said to the others. 'I'll see which one looks the most interesting.'

'Sure,' said John. 'Hey, look. What do you suppose this is?' He pulled an ancient leather hoop from the tangle on a stall and poked his head through it.

'Is for a horse,' said the man behind the stall, smiling to reveal several missing teeth. 'Twenty euros, OK?'

John shook his head as the others laughed. Maxine wandered off towards the row of shops and bars that lined the marketplace. She couldn't understand why her friends didn't want to explore the little town. This might easily be the only chance they had.

She reached the entrance to a narrow street, cool in the shadow of the tall buildings on either side. At the end of the street was a small sunlit square where a fountain played in the shade of a small tree. It looked perfect. She turned back to go and tell the others, and then she stopped.

Courtney was walking along the pavement towards her. At least, it looked like Courtney, but she was wearing a red and white scarf over her head and she had on jeans and a T-shirt. Courtney would never wear anything so ordinary.

Then Maxine recognized the T-shirt. It was one of Danny's, with a picture of Michael Jackson on the front. It was Courtney, for sure, and it almost looked as if she was wearing some kind of disguise!

Maxine flattened herself into a doorway as she passed, then followed her along the crowded pavement and saw her vanish into a café. She was almost certain that Courtney wouldn't recognize any of the athletes from Camp Gold, so she took a chance and sat down at one of the tables outside. A waiter appeared and Maxine ordered a

Coke. It seemed to be the same word in Spanish, or was it Catalan?

She risked a glance inside. Courtney was seated at a table by the bar, and she was deep in conversation with a bald-headed man wearing a dark suit. The man seemed to be doing most of the talking, and whatever Courtney was saying in reply didn't seem to please him. There was definitely a mystery here. Maxine swallowed her Coke, left the money on the table and hurried back to the market to fetch the others.

'It's her,' she told them breathlessly as she led them back to the café. 'And she didn't want anyone to know she was meeting this man.'

'So, where is she then?' asked John, leading the way towards the café door.

'No, wait,' said Maxine. 'We can't all go bursting in there. We can't stand outside and look in, either. She'll know something's up.'

'You're right,' agreed John. 'I'll just take a

peek, OK?' He sidled up to the door and glanced inside, then turned back to the others with a shrug. 'There's nobody,' he said.

'There must be,' said Maxine. But when she looked, the little café was empty.

'I keep telling you,' said John, 'there's no mystery about Courtney. She—'

'There!' interrupted Maxine, pointing eagerly. 'You see that car? That's him. That's the man she was talking to.'

A low, sleek black car had emerged from a street a few metres away and they all had a clear view of the man's profile – a long nose and a jutting jaw – before he swung the car out into the square, honking the horn impatiently to clear the shoppers out of his way.

'Wow! A Mercedes CLS,' said John, his eyes bright as he watched the shiny car vanish down the street. 'That is one expensive automobile!'

'Don't look at the car,' said Maxine. 'There's

Courtney! I told you, there's something going on.'

Courtney was walking away from them, but even in her different clothes, her walk – a fashion model's wiggle of the hips – was unmistakable.

'How can she do this?' demanded Sasha, her green eyes flashing angrily. 'How can she two-time him? She is Danny's girlfriend. How can she treat him like this?'

John turned to Sasha. 'I bet there's a perfectly reasonable explanation. She's a model, after all. She must have to meet people for her work. And maybe she doesn't want the press following her around. That's probably why she wore that disguise.'

'You are crazy,' said Sasha. 'She loves it when they take her picture. You saw her at the airport.' She narrowed her eyes. 'I'm certain something is going on. We should watch her very carefully from now on.'

CHAPTER SIX

The next day was Friday, the day of the first mini-competition at Camp Gold International. The athletes did some light training in the morning and had the rest of the day free until the competition in the evening. Maxine and her friends went to the basketball court after training, but soon realized that it was too hot for anything more strenuous than a little gentle shooting practice.

'It does not matter,' said Sasha. 'We can see her – that is the most important thing.'

Through a screen of slender tree trunks they could see the swimming pool, and beside it, stretched out on sun-loungers, lay Courtney and Danny.

'We could watch a lot more easily if we just went for a swim,' John pointed out, flinging a lazy underarm shot at the basket. The ball dropped though the hoop without touching it.

'We do not want her to know we are watching her,' Sasha said dramatically. 'We must not arouse her suspicions. Look, Danny is like her slave. She is horrible.'

They watched as Danny stood up, walked to the far end of the pool and returned with an iced drink for Courtney. She said something to him and he turned and repeated his journey, returning with two straws.

John shook his head and laughed. 'You stay

here if you like. You guys are imagining all kinds of things. She's a crazy fashion model, and that's all she is, if you ask me. I'm going for a swim. Anyone coming?' He strolled off towards the pool with Hiari, leaving Jade, Maxine and Sasha sitting in the shade of the wall.

'Do you think you might win this afternoon?' Maxine asked Sasha.

'Yes, of course,' replied Sasha without taking her eyes off Courtney. 'There is a girl called Diane from Australia, though. Look, you can see her in the pool. It is her I will have to beat.'

They all watched as a tall girl with cropped blonde hair and a deep brown body somersaulted from the diving board and entered the water without a splash.

Sasha nodded in grudging admiration. 'She is good, but I think I will win,' she said. 'How about you, Maxine?'

'I don't think so,' Maxine replied gloomily.
'My times are way off at the moment. Jade's
running far better than me.'

'And Hiari is the best,' Jade added. 'She never
even looks tired at the end of a race. I don't think
I'll ever beat her.'

Sasha turned to her, her face suddenly serious.
'Of course you will,' she said. 'You have to
believe this. You too, Maxine. If you think like
this you are beaten before you start. I always
believe I am going to win.'

Jade looked at Maxine and they both burst out
laughing. 'I do not understand,' Sasha
complained. 'What is the joke?'

'Nothing,' said Maxine, through tears of
laughter. 'You're absolutely right.'

The competition took place that evening on a
floodlit track. 'The event in the Olympic
Stadium will be held in the evening,' Kath had

told them, 'so you should get used to competing at this time of day.'

There was even a small crowd of spectators at the side of the track as the contest got underway. Many of the staff who helped to run Camp Gold had stayed on to watch, and among them Maxine noticed Rosalita. She was talking to John in a very animated fashion and Maxine wondered what they were talking about.

'She likes him,' Jade said in Maxine's ear. 'That's easy to see. But he shouldn't be standing there talking. He's in one of the first races.'

John suddenly remembered this and hurried off to the warm-up area. The distraction didn't seem to do him any harm. Fifteen minutes later he won his 400-metre race in a time that was very close to a record for his age group. He joined Maxine, Hiari and Jade by the side of the track, flushed with triumph.

'What did Rosalita want?' Maxine enquired.

'Oh, nothing,' replied John, and Maxine was almost sure that he blushed slightly. 'I'll tell you later. We should go and watch Sasha. She's next up after this.'

They walked over to the pole-vault run-up just in time to see Sasha's rival, Diane, race down the runway and curve through the air, clearing the bar with almost a metre to spare. 'She's good, isn't she,' said John admiringly.

'So is Sasha,' replied Maxine as her friend rocked back and forth one last time before accelerating towards them. The bar looked impossibly high, but Sasha took off perfectly and cleared it by almost as much as Diane. The friends cheered wildly and Sasha turned and gave them a thumbs-up; then, as she walked back to her friends, her face darkened and Maxine turned to see what she was staring at.

Danny Crowe was standing near the track and Courtney was beside him; she was looking supremely bored with what was going on around her. Danny said something to her, indicating the pole-vaulter who was soaring into the air at that moment. Courtney gave a little pout and walked away, back towards the main buildings.

'Good riddance,' said Sasha. 'I do not want her watching me.'

'I thought we were meant to be watching her,' Maxine said.

'True,' replied Sasha. 'You should follow.'

'Not us,' said Jade. 'We have to warm up.'

'Don't look at me,' said John. 'You know I think you're all mad. There's no way she's up to anything, and I think your coach wants you, Sasha.'

As Maxine went through her warm-up routine she could already feel the tension building inside her. It had been there in the background all day, but now it really kicked in. Her shoulders and neck were stiff and she felt as if a cold hand was lying on her stomach. She tried to think of Sasha. She tried, like Sasha, to believe that she would win, but when she looked around and saw Hui Zhong and Jerry, Jade and Hiari, it was impossible to convince herself that she was good enough. Then she caught Martha giving her an unpleasant look and she knew that she still suspected her of going through her bag. That made her feel even worse.

Kath called the runners out onto the track. There would be two races and Maxine was running in the first of them. These were the runners with the eight fastest personal bests, and Maxine knew well enough that the four girls she had just watched warming up were all faster than her. She tried to put that hard fact out of her mind as they raced round the first bend, but as they broke for pole position with Hiari already moving smoothly into the lead, it looked as if the race would run true to form.

As they began the second and final lap Hiari was leading a group of four. Hui Zhong was at her shoulder, with Jade and Jerry right behind them. Then there was a two-metre gap to where Maxine led the other runners, a Japanese girl named Yuriko almost on her shoulder. She gritted her teeth and pushed hard to prevent the gap from growing bigger. She succeeded, and as they approached the final bend she was still within striking distance of the leading group. There was a brief, thrilling moment as they entered the final straight when she thought that she might be able to overtake all of them, surprising them down the outside, but then, suddenly, they were running away from her as Hiari accelerated explosively and the others responded.

There was nothing Maxine could do but watch as Jade moved past Hui Zhong and Jerry and almost caught Hiari on the line. Maxine finished fifth, with Martha nearly catching her on the line. She had run as fast as she knew how, but it hadn't been good enough. She said so to Danny when he came over and congratulated her on a gritty performance.

'I should be able to go faster,' she said. 'But I just can't . . .'

'Don't worry,' Danny replied. 'Look at it this way: you're less than half a second from being the best in the world for your age. All you have to do is find that half a second. That's why you're here.'

Danny was about to say more when Courtney appeared. 'I'm ready to leave now,' she said with a pout. 'You don't have to stay any longer, darling, do you?'

'Well, I just want to say a few words to these girls,' Danny replied. 'Didn't you see that race? They were awesome!'

Courtney muttered something under her breath, and then waited impatiently as Danny spoke to the other 800-metre runners. Maxine was relieved to know that Danny wasn't totally under Courtney's thumb, and the smile on Jade's face when Danny congratulated her on her performance was something to see.

Danny went off with Courtney and the girls made their way to the locker room. The moment she unzipped her bag, Maxine had a feeling that something was wrong. Her spare T-shirt that had been neatly folded in the bottom of the bag was now lying crumpled on the top, as though it had been thrust into the bag in a hurry. She pulled everything out. No, it was all there. She showered and dressed and went to put on the glittery bracelet that Joshua had given her for luck at the airport. She felt a sudden panic as she realized that it wasn't there, and she pulled everything out of the bag again, searching everywhere.

It was the last straw. She burst into tears, and a few moments later Jade emerged from the showers and found her crying.

'What is it?' asked Jade, putting an arm around her. 'What's happened?'

Maxine explained about the bracelet and they searched through her things again together. 'I shouldn't have taken it off,' she said tearfully. 'I told Joshua I'd wear it in every race and I completely forgot. Now look what's happened. I'm almost sure that someone has been looking in my bag. Everything was messed up. But why would anyone steal that bracelet? It's not as if it was worth anything to anyone but me.'

'I don't know,' began Jade, bending to take clothes from her own bag. Then she paused. 'You know what?' she said. 'I think this has been searched too.' She picked up a spectacles case. 'I know I packed this away in the bottom.'

'Right,' said Jerry from the opposite side of the room. 'I reckon someone's been in here and gone through all the bags. Mine's messed up too.'

'I told you,' Martha said angrily. 'But you wouldn't believe me.'

'Yeah, well maybe now you'll believe that it wasn't me,' said Maxine.

Outside, they found John waiting with a similar story. They could hear angry voices coming from the boys' locker room.

'I've told the others I'll go and see Michael,' John said. 'You should come too, Maxine. But first we have to watch the end of the pole-vault. Everything else has finished, but Sasha and Diane are still going strong.'

A sizeable crowd had gathered to watch the closing stages of the pole-vault, which was reaching a nail-biting climax. Both Sasha and Diane had two failures against their names and both had an equal number of clearances. Sasha had already achieved two new PBs and the bar was now higher than either girl had ever vaulted before.

Diane was on the runway. She set off, planted her pole firmly and climbed into the air. As she curled over the bar the hem of her shorts made the tiniest contact and the bar vibrated for a long moment like the string of a guitar. As Diane landed in the pit she looked up anxiously, but the bar stayed put, balanced right on the edge of the supports. There was loud applause from the crowd, followed by a silence broken only by the chirruping of crickets as Sasha began her approach.

Her vault was almost identical to Diane's. Sasha's shorts, too, set the bar vibrating. The crowd watched, hearts in mouths, as it hovered for an age . . . before tumbling down. Sasha punched the foam of the landing pad with her fist, then leaped up smiling and shook Diane's hand.

'Next time the bar will stay on for me too,' she told Maxine, Jade and John when she joined them a little later. 'But something has happened. Everyone is talking about it. Tell me.'

After they had explained to Sasha she was eager to check her own bag, and when she emerged from the locker room her face was red with anger. 'We will go and see Michael right now,' she said. 'This is too bad.'

'You know, it's weird – no one has actually stolen anything,' John said as they made their way to the office area in the new building. 'Not even when they broke into Michael's office.'

'What about my bracelet?' demanded Maxine. 'I know I had it before the race and it's definitely gone.'

'Wait a minute,' said Jade. 'What's that?'

They all stopped and stared in astonishment. There, on the floor of the corridor, was Maxine's precious bracelet. She bent and picked it up. 'How could it possibly have got here?' she asked, fixing it firmly onto her wrist.

'This is all very strange,' said Sasha, crossing the corridor to knock on Michael's door. 'I do not like it at all.'

As Michael called for them to come in, Maxine glanced around at the other doors. All had the names of their occupants on white labels. Kath had an office, and Danny, and several of the other coaches too. Why would any of them have dropped Maxine's bracelet there?

'Come on,' said John. 'Michael's waiting.'

Michael was sitting behind his desk. He was frowning, and looking more anxious than Maxine had ever seen him before. Last year he had joined in the basketball games every night. He and Danny had been a part of everything, but this year they had hardly seen Michael, and Danny — well, Danny had Courtney to think about.

John explained their suspicions about their bags being searched and the others backed him up.

'I heard people muttering about it down at the track,' Michael said. 'Are you sure you couldn't be mistaken?'

'We're sure,' said Maxine, uncertain whether to mention finding her bracelet right outside. 'It's happened before too. There was Sasha's room, remember, and your office.'

'I know,' said Michael. 'Listen, I feel like I'm letting you all down. You should be having a good time and concentrating on your training. You're all doing amazingly well under the circumstances. That was a fantastic performance tonight, Sasha. Thrilling! And you others were terrific too. Leave this problem with me. We'll find a way to sort it out, I promise you.'

CHAPTER SEVEN

'I think we all need to get out of this place and have some fun,' said John later that evening.

Maxine, Jade, Hiari and Sasha were all sitting with him on the terrace of the restaurant. The sky above them was covered in stars. The warm air was full of the scent of pine trees and the sound of crickets.

'What are you talking about?' asked Maxine

suspiciously. 'You've thought of something, haven't you?'

'It was Rosalita who thought of it,' said John, and Maxine wondered if he was blushing in the darkness. 'She invited all of us to go to the fiesta tomorrow afternoon with her family.'

'Are you sure it wasn't only you she invited?' asked Sasha mischievously.

'No,' replied John. 'She meant all of us. And we can do it easily. There's no training tomorrow afternoon, remember? We just have light training in the morning to loosen up after the competition, but we don't have the usual training session in the early evening. It's only three kilometres into town, so we can just say we're going for a walk up the trail. As long as we're back before they lock the gates when it gets dark no one will ever know we were gone. It'll be like last year. We had a good time, didn't we?'

'We got caught,' Maxine pointed out. 'They almost threw us out.'

'But they didn't,' said Sasha. 'And John is right. Why would anyone know where we have been? It is very exciting.'

'I don't know,' said Jade, a little anxiously. 'You lot did get in trouble last year.'

For most of the time they had been at Camp Gold the year before, Jade had been Maxine's bitter rival and she hadn't been part of her group of friends. Jade had missed out on the beach party, but Maxine couldn't help remembering how wonderful it had been, even if they had paid for it afterwards.

'I think it'll be OK,' Maxine said finally, in spite of the nagging doubt she still felt. 'We have been invited, after all, and it's not as if we aren't allowed out of Camp Gold at all.'

'Well, OK,' said Jade. 'How about you, Hiari?'

'For sure,' agreed Hiari, and her teeth gleamed

white in the darkness as she smiled. 'I don't want to miss a thing.'

They were making their way a little nervously out of the main entrance the following afternoon when they saw Michael and Isabel standing in the shade of the small gatehouse as if they were waiting for somebody. Maxine's heart gave a flutter, but she told herself that they were doing nothing wrong.

'Are you crazy?' asked Michael when he saw them approaching. 'Going for a walk at this time of day?'

'We're going into the woods,' John said, indicating the dark band of pine trees that hugged the top of the cliffs. 'It'll be cool there.'

'True,' Michael nodded, looking distractedly at his watch and glancing at Isabel. 'Make sure you stick to the trail. Remember the gates are locked at dusk.'

'OK,' said Maxine. 'Thanks, Michael. We won't be late.'

Her voice sounded false in her ears, but Michael was obviously thinking about something else, and the small group of friends hurried away up the rocky trail towards the woods. When they reached the edge of the trees they looked back and saw that a blue car had pulled up by the entrance and a tall, white-suited man was shaking Michael's hand.

'It is another mystery,' said Sasha. 'Something is going on and we must find out everything!'

'How about we just get to the fiesta?' sighed John. 'You see mysteries everywhere, Sasha. We'll follow the trees until we're out of sight and then we can go back down to the road.' Maxine laughed – John seemed to have no imagination and Sasha far too much!

John set off along the path. They paused at the top of the rise and looked back again. The car, and Michael and Isabel, had gone. They descended to the road and walked along its dusty edge between the fields as a steady stream of vehicles passed them: trucks, buses, cars of every shape and size, all packed with people. They were still some distance from the town when they heard the music.

'I can smell food!' said Hiari. 'And it smells delicious.'

Even in the afternoon heat, the mouth-watering aromas gave them the energy to hurry and, as they entered the town, the narrow streets were filling up with people making for the main square. When they reached it they saw that stalls selling food had been set up all around the edge, but the paved centre of the square had been cleared and a stage erected on a farm trailer at the far side. There were flags everywhere, and music blared from loudspeakers hung from lampposts and buildings.

'We have to find Rosalita's house,' John yelled in Maxine's ear above the noise. 'I've got the address written down here.' He waved a piece of paper under her nose. *Calle de la Iglesia 14* was written on it in neat, curly handwriting.

'That's easy,' said Maxine, recognizing the name. 'I know where it is, come on.' She led the way across the square to the narrow street with the fountain at the end of it where she had been hoping to explore before she had spotted Courtney on their previous visit to the town. 'See?' she said, pointing to the sign on the wall. 'It's down here.'

As they walked down the street they saw that behind the fountain in the square, a flight of steps ran up to the massive doors of a church.

'Of course,' said John. '*Iglesia* means church. This is Church Street.' They paused outside the door of number fourteen and John knocked. The door opened and the space was filled by a large, smiling man. 'Er, *buenos días*,' stammered John. '*Es . . . es Rosalita aquí?*'

Maxine thought John was brave. She wasn't much good at French at school and she wasn't sure she would have dared to try speaking Spanish. John had obviously been practising.

'He is trying to impress Rosalita,' whispered Sasha, raising her eyebrows.

'Ah!' said the man, his smile becoming even wider as he was joined by several wide-eyed children, including one very small boy who thrust his head between his father's legs. '*Hablas español? Muy bien!* Rosalita! Your friends are here. You see?' he said, turning back to the visitors. 'I speak excellent English myself, no? Come in, come in! We will eat and then we will go to watch the procession.'

Rosalita's family melted away into the dark interior, leaving Rosalita standing there, smiling shyly, with just the smallest boy clinging to her leg. Maxine suddenly felt a pang of homesickness and looked down to check that Joshua's bracelet was still on her wrist. Rosalita led them through the house and out into a shaded courtyard, where they sat around a huge wooden table and tucked into a feast of chicken and rice and peppers and all kinds of wonderfully prepared vegetables. They were finishing the meal by nibbling at some delicious and very moreish custard tarts – as well as a plateful of the gloriously chocolaty churros they had tried before – when they heard the sound of a band striking up in the street outside.

'We must hurry,' said Rosalita. 'We do not want to miss the procession. Come on.'

'But we should help to clear up,' said Maxine, gazing at the vast amount of washing-up they had created.

Rosalita's mother said something very firmly in Spanish – or probably Catalan, Maxine reminded herself. 'Go! Go!' exclaimed her father, making as if to shoo them out of the house with his enormous hands. 'You must see everything. Ours is the finest fiesta in all of Catalonia. No! In all of Spain!'

They found themselves propelled out onto the street and instantly came face to face with the head of a large green dragon, bobbing back and forth to the harsh music of trumpets and drums, and instruments that Maxine thought might be oboes. The dragon was followed by a large group of dancers wearing grotesque heads with white faces and distorted features. The heads made the dancers look incredibly tall as they cavorted down the street. They were followed by a band of military drummers. The noise echoed between the walls, deafening them.

'Come on,' cried Rosalita, grabbing Maxine's hand. 'We must follow!'

The friends from Camp Gold were swept up

into the procession and whirled onwards into the square by the little church, and then through a maze of streets. Overwhelmed by the music and dizzy from the dancing, Maxine lost all track of where she was, but then, quite suddenly, she saw the car.

It was parked in a side street: the same black, shiny Mercedes that Courtney's mysterious friend had been driving. Maxine yelled to John through the crowd and pointed over the sea of heads, but it was no good. They were carried forward by the crowd and she lost sight of it.

'You can't be sure it was the same one,' John said, when she finally got close enough to shout into his ear.

'I can. I remember the numberplate,' she retorted. 'It began with eight-eight-eight-four.'

And then, before John could reply, they all emerged into the square and there was another deafening blast of trumpeting from a group of men nearby. Wild music continued and another group began a strange dance involving some kind of sticks. It looked weirdly familiar to Maxine, and then she remembered. 'It's like Morris dancing,' she said to Jade, who was standing beside her. 'I've seen it in the park at home.'

But Jade was staring over her shoulder. 'It's Courtney,' she said breathlessly. 'She's right over there, on the other side of the dancers. She's talking to that man.'

Maxine turned and followed Jade's gaze. They couldn't see the man's face, but she could tell from the way he was standing and the way he was jabbing his finger at Courtney that he was very angry indeed. Maxine quickly drew the attention of John, Sasha and Hiari to the scene that was playing out just a few metres away. Rosalita saw them all watching, and looked puzzled.

Courtney was scared, decided Maxine. She flinched away from every angry jab of the man's finger. Watching her, Maxine felt a sudden, unexpected pang of sympathy. Courtney looked like a frightened little girl.

The man turned suddenly and pushed his way through the crowd, drawing sharp cries of complaint as he went. Courtney hesitated for a moment, then followed in his wake. The friends looked at each other.

'Do you still think he's her boyfriend?' Maxine asked Sasha.

Sasha shook her head. 'No,' she said. 'But I like this even less. She is in some kind of trouble, I think.'

They all agreed about that. 'I know this woman,' Rosalita said, and Maxine was startled by the look of hatred on her face. 'She treats all of us like dirt. All of us who work at your Camp Gold. She is a very bad person, I think. You should forget her. This way. We must watch the dancing.' She pointed to the stage, where lights had been switched on and a large troupe of dancers were weaving out to a clattering of castanets and the insistent beat of drums. 'It is good, no?' demanded Rosalita. 'The best in Spain!'

But Sasha was looking at the dazzling spotlights with a horrified expression. 'The lights!' she said. 'It is getting dark!'

'It can't be.' Maxine stared at her watch. 'How did it get to be this time?' Her watch told her that it was nearly eight o'clock, but it was impossible to believe.

'It's not too late,' said John. 'The sun's gone behind those hills, but it doesn't set for a while yet. We can get back in time, but we'll have to run.'

'We'll never get through these crowds,' said Jade, her face pale with alarm.

'I show you the way,' interrupted Rosalita.
'Come!'

She led them quickly to the edge of the square, and then on through a network of alleyways to the edge of town.

'Hey, you can run fast,' said Maxine.

'*Sí*,' said Rosalita, breathing hard, 'but not like you, I think. I see you later.'

They jogged off up the road, and as they drew nearer to Camp Gold the road climbed out of the valley. They ran in single file, without speaking, as the sun shone out suddenly from beneath a long line of ragged black cloud, sending their long shadows dancing out across the rocky landscape in a flood of orange light.

When they were almost up to the gates John slowed. 'We should walk the last bit,' he said. 'We've been for a picnic in the woods, remember?'

Maxine stopped, looking at the line of

shadows; then she turned to the others. 'Where's Hiari?' she said.

They all stared at each other. 'I thought she was behind me,' Sasha said. 'I never looked.'

'We've still got some time,' said John. 'She's probably still watching the dancing. She was loving it. We'll have to go back and fetch her.'

'Not all of us,' said Maxine. 'I'll go. Maybe you can distract Juan somehow. Stop him closing the gates. I'll be as quick as I can.'

Without giving them any chance to argue, she took off back down the road towards the town.

CHAPTER EIGHT

Maxine ran fast. There was no thought in her mind of setting a sensible pace. She had to get Hiari back before the gates closed, and she was going to do it. She ran into the last rays of the sun, and then, as the road dropped into the wide valley, she ran on in the gathering dusk towards the twinkling lights of the town, thinking how lucky it was that there were no cars on the road. When she reached it she jogged quickly up the narrow main street, but as she turned a corner massive shadowy figures loomed towards her.

She halted and pressed herself back against the wall as fiery torches threw great flickering shadows ahead of the figures. Then suddenly she laughed with relief as she recognized the grotesque white faces of the dancers she had seen earlier, and there, following the dancers, she saw a very worried-looking Hiari.

'Hiari!' she called. 'Over here! Hurry!'

Hiari searched the darkness for the source of the voice, then saw Maxine and her face relaxed into a smile of relief as she pushed through the crowd towards her.

'I'm sorry,' Maxine said. 'We thought you were with us.'

'It's OK,' replied Hiari. 'I was having fun.'

Maxine knew that wasn't true, but she said nothing. 'We have to run,' she said. 'I don't know if we'll make it. We have to go as fast as we can.'

The dancers had turned off into an alleyway and the main street was empty again as the music and shouting faded away. They could hear the booming of a band on the stage in the square as they turned and raced down the hill and out into the countryside.

'If a car comes we'll see their lights and get off the road, OK?' panted Maxine.

Hiari nodded agreement, and after that neither girl had any breath to spare for talking. They settled into a steady rhythm as they ran side by side up the deserted road in the growing darkness. From time to time Maxine glanced across at Hiari, but she seemed to be lost in a world of her own. Her stride never faltered and Maxine could tell that running was as natural to Hiari as breathing.

They were out of the valley now, and they could see the dark outline of the castle tower. As Maxine watched, a light came on, and then another. Without exchanging a word the girls increased their pace, but when they were still several hundred metres away they saw the gates sliding shut.

They stopped running and looked at each other in horror, but it was some time before either of them could speak. 'What now?' asked Hiari.

Maxine shook her head. She had no idea. As they stood helplessly by the side of the road they heard the sound of a car's engine. 'Over there, quick,' urged Maxine, and they scrambled up behind some boulders on the opposite side of the road.

'Why?' asked Hiari.

'I just don't think we should let anyone see us out here. That car might be Michael. We don't know.'

They waited. The twin beams of headlights raked across the sky and then the car came into sight. It slowed and stopped by the gates. The door opened and Courtney stepped out, illuminated from behind by the lights on top of the gate pillars. They heard a man's voice. 'Make sure this time. If you don't . . .' Courtney bent down to the car window and said something that they couldn't hear. The man's voice cut her off. 'I don't care. You wanted this . . .'

The car suddenly accelerated away, forcing Courtney to stand up sharply. She tottered backwards and almost fell before walking quickly to the gate and pressing the buzzer. The gates slid open and she walked in.

'Why can't we do that?' asked Hiari. 'We can just say we went for a walk and got lost and we're a bit late getting back.'

Maxine shook her head. 'Michael wouldn't accept that,' she said. 'We'd be in serious trouble.'

'I'm sorry,' said Hiari. 'It is my fault. I should have realized—'

Maxine's phone buzzed in her pocket and she pulled it out. There was a text from John. Relief washed over her as she read it.

'It's all right,' she said happily, looking up at Hiari. 'We can get back in.' She put the phone away, very glad that her mum had bought her extra credit and insisted that she keep the phone switched on all the time.

'How?' demanded Hiari.

'Oh, sorry. Rosalita has told John there's a place where the local kids get through the fence when there's nobody here and they want to go swimming. All we have to do is find it.'

'But there are miles of fence.'

'John told me which way to go. He's going to meet us. Come on, let's get moving.'

They slipped quickly across the road. There was still enough light in the western sky for them to avoid the rocks and boulders that lay around outside the fence, but as they neared the area close to the running track they entered a small copse of pine trees and the going became more difficult. Hiari yelped with pain as a branch scraped her cheek, but Maxine hushed her. There was another sound from somewhere inside Camp Gold.

'What was that?' asked Hiari, rubbing her cheek.

'I'm not sure,' replied Maxine. 'John said he'd—' They heard the sound again, this time from very close by, and Maxine had to stifle a giggle. 'I think that was supposed to be an owl,' she said.

'It sounded more like a crow,' said Hiari, laughing too.

'John,' hissed Maxine, moving closer to the fence. 'Over here.'

Shadowy forms appeared inside the fence. John was there, and so were Jade and Sasha. 'Sorry about the owl,' said John. 'The hole is just down here. It's not very big and you'll have to move those rocks. I've cleared them from this side.'

At her feet Maxine could just make out a jumble of small boulders lying at the foot of the fence. With Hiari's assistance she began to roll them away to reveal a narrow gap under the fence. 'Don't move them too far,' John warned. 'We have to reach under and pull them back into place when we've finished. Otherwise someone's bound to find the hole.'

First Hiari, then Maxine squeezed under the fence to be reunited with the others, before carefully hiding the entrance again. They were safely back inside Camp Gold!

'We didn't know what to do,' Maxine said as they walked back through the grounds. 'We thought we were done for. It's lucky I had my phone. But listen, we saw Courtney . . .'

She quickly filled the others in on the scene

they had witnessed outside the gates. This time even John couldn't think of a sensible explanation.

'If she wasn't Danny's girlfriend I would tell Michael about this right now,' said Sasha. 'It is very creepy.'

Maxine found herself walking beside Hiari as the others moved on ahead, discussing Maxine's news. 'You ran a long way tonight,' Hiari said.

Maxine hadn't even thought about it. 'I suppose.'

'You did. You ran back with the others, then back into town to find me, and then we ran back together. And we ran fast. Very fast.'

'I enjoyed it,' Maxine said.

'Me too. I love running. When I used to run to school and back it was always the best time of the day.'

'I used to be like that,' Maxine said, a little sadly. 'Last year, when I first found out it was what I really wanted to do, I loved every minute of it. But now . . .'

'Every race we have run you looked as if you were fighting something,' Hiari said. 'But not tonight. Tonight you were running like a wild horse.'

Maxine didn't reply. Now that she considered what she had done she realized that it was true. She had run three times as far as Hiari, yet she had kept up with her easily. If only she could do that in a race! She was so involved in her thoughts that she almost walked right into Jade, who had stopped suddenly along with the others.

'I thought I saw a light,' John whispered. 'Over there in the small gym.'

There were several gyms on the Camp Gold site. This one was situated near the running track and had a sauna and a small pool attached to it. Everything was in darkness, but then a small part of the darkness seemed to detach itself from the rest and a shadow moved stealthily away from the building into the shelter of some trees.

'What was it?' breathed Jade. 'Or who?'

'I don't know,' replied John. 'We should investigate. Come on.'

They walked quickly over to the building, John reached for the handle and the door swung open. He stepped inside and felt for the light switch. The sudden glare hurt Maxine's eyes after so long in the dark. She heard a gasp, and opened her eyes to a scene of devastation. On her right the door to the locker room was open. Lockers were open and their contents spilled onto the floor. Items from the medical cupboard were scattered everywhere. Inside the gym it was the same thing. Store cupboards stood open and their contents piled in a jumbled mess.

The friends were all too astonished to do anything other than stare in disbelief. They were still staring when the door opened behind them.

'What the—?' Michael stood in the doorway, a look of horrified anger on his face. 'Why would you do this? Why?'

'But we didn't,' said John, his face flushing. 'We spotted a light and then we saw someone running from the building. We thought we should find out what was going on.'

'That's kind of lame, don't you think, John?' said Michael, looking disgusted. 'You guys are wandering around out here in the dark and then you just happen to see a light? I don't think so.'

Sasha stepped forward angrily. 'We would never do something like this,' she said. 'You know we would not. We may do foolish things sometimes, but we do not do bad things. I give you my word – we never touched any of this.'

'It's true,' Maxine burst out. 'Why would we

do something like this? It was nothing to do with us.'

'OK,' said Michael slowly, looking at each of their faces in turn. 'Maybe this isn't down to you. But you were up to something. I know you, remember?'

There was a brief, awkward pause. 'We have to tell him,' Maxine said, unable to bear the tension any longer.

'OK,' said Sasha. 'But you must promise you won't send us home,' she added to Michael.

'I'm not going to promise you a thing,' he said. 'Come on, spit it out. What have you been doing?'

'We went into town,' Maxine admitted. 'We went to the fiesta.'

'We had an invitation,' John added. 'Rosalita's family invited us. We went to their house and had a meal with them.'

'They think Camp Gold is wonderful,' Jade

said. 'They've got tickets for the Olympic Stadium and everything.'

'Stop!' said Michael. 'Enough! I don't suppose it occurred to any of you that if you'd just asked us, we might have let you go? Then you wouldn't have had to make up stories about going for a walk in the woods.'

Sasha started to say something but Michael held up his hand. 'I know what you're going to say, Sasha. You did go for a walk. You just went a bit further than the woods, right? You shouldn't have done it, and you know it, don't you?'

They all nodded. Michael looked at them and shook his head. 'Isabel reckons I'm too soft,' he said. 'But I know you're not bad kids . . .'

Maxine started to smile. 'I haven't finished,' Michael went on. 'You've had your trip out now. There were two more outings planned for you, so you can stay here when the others go, and you can do extra training. Fair enough? You guys should be setting an example. You know what we expect from you, right?'

'Yes, Michael,' they all said.

'All right. We'll say no more about it, but don't step out of line again. Now, you say you saw someone running away? Did you recognize them?'

Suddenly Maxine thought of Courtney. She would have had time, but why? Why would she do such a thing? Certainly the man in the car had wanted her to do something, but not this, surely? The shape she had half seen flitting from the door could have been Courtney, but it could have been almost anyone.

'It was dark,' said John. 'We really couldn't see.'

'Pity,' said Michael, turning to stare at the mess. 'Well, here's a little extra punishment for you. You can help me tidy this lot up. And when I find out who's behind this, they really *will* be going home.'

CHAPTER NINE

The next morning all the athletes had an early start, and when Maxine arrived at the track she found that all the coaches were in a sombre mood.

'You all know what happened last night,' Kath said. 'From now on, no one is to go to the locker rooms alone. We're going to put a stop to this nonsense. It's gone beyond a joke, way beyond.'

There was a long silence. Maxine looked

around at the other athletes. It was impossible to imagine any of them doing anything so stupid, so destructive. It wasn't as if anything had been taken. As far as she knew, her bracelet was the only thing that had been stolen so far, and she had found it again almost immediately.

Yet again, her thoughts turned to Courtney. The girls had all discussed her the night before, when they had finally finished tidying the gym and made their way a little wearily back up the stone stairs into the tower.

Standing on the landing outside Hiari's room, Sasha had been surprisingly level-headed. 'We have watched her, but we have seen nothing. We have nothing but suspicions. It is useless to accuse her if we cannot prove it.'

'I know,' Maxine had replied, 'but you all saw her with that man. Something is going on. She's in some kind of trouble. Don't you think we should at least tell Danny?'

'I don't think Danny would like that,' said Jade slowly. 'I mean, it would sound like we've been spying on her. And we have been. He probably wouldn't believe us, anyway.'

'We will keep watching,' Sasha said. 'At least Michael believed us when we told him it wasn't us. We are very lucky, I think.'

They had all agreed about that. But Maxine didn't regret going to the fiesta, not for one moment. It had been awesome, and the best bit had been running back in the dark with Hiari.

'Right, then,' said Kath. 'I'm going to take the distance runners for a long run through the hills. Maybe it'll remind some of you that running can be fun as well as hard work.'

As they set off out of the gate, Maxine wondered if Kath had been reading her mind. They started up the same path they had followed the day before when they had pretended to be going for a picnic, but when they reached the trees Kath continued up the trail as it wound uphill through sparse woodland between rocks and sweet-smelling bushes.

Maxine ran with Hiari. Ahead of them she could see Jade chatting animatedly to Hui Zhong as they jogged along. Three large black birds circled in the sky. 'They're black kites,' Hiari said. 'I saw them yesterday from the terrace and asked Rosalita. This run is good. Makes a change from all the hard work.'

'You never look as if it is hard work,' Maxine replied.

'No? Well, it is. I want to win a gold medal at the Olympics. And I want to carry that torch too. Jade nearly beat me the other day, and I reckon you could too.'

'I don't think so. Not the way I've been running lately.'

Hiari glanced sideways at her. 'Have you forgotten last night? I have never run faster.

I seriously did not want to get in trouble. And you kept up with me all the way. You've got me worried, truly. I am going to work harder than ever. Hey, look! Rabbits!'

Maxine laughed. It was great to be out here in the countryside, and whatever else happened at Camp Gold International this summer, she knew she had found a new friend in Hiari.

As the week went on the pace and intensity of the training increased; on Tuesday morning Kath told them that Kerry Jones, currently the world's fastest 800-metre runner, would be joining them for the weekend, and would be there to watch their end-of-week competition, which had been moved to Saturday evening this week so that she could be there – the coaches valued her opinion.

Maxine felt a rush of nervous excitement, and at once her imagination went into fevered overdrive. What if she suddenly found her form again and managed to defeat Hiari and Jade and all the others? She pictured herself crossing the line, throwing her arms into the air as Kerry Jones looked on. But that wasn't going to happen. She was bound to mess it up again. She looked at the others and saw to her relief that they were as anxious as she was. She ought not to be so worried. After all, Danny Crowe was even more famous than Kerry Jones. But Danny seemed like an old friend now, and Kerry Jones was right at the top in Maxine's own event.

'That is scary,' said Hiari, beside her. 'Imagine running in front of her.'

'My legs will be like jelly,' said Jade, and all the others nodded agreement.

Kath laughed. 'Good!' she said. 'Have you forgotten that you'll be running in front of fifty thousand people in two weeks' time. You may as well get used to being nervous.'

Over the next few days, training went well for Maxine. Kath continued to take the distance runners for early-morning runs through the hills and woods. For Maxine these runs were the best part of the day, and gradually she found herself enjoying the hard work too. She even went for the optional early-morning run on their rest day, Thursday, as she was enjoying them so much! And she and her friends got in some extra training runs when – as part of the punishment Michael had imposed for their trip out to the fiesta – they missed an excursion the other athletes were bussed out for one evening.

In sprints and interval training she was comfortably keeping up with the others, and for the first time since she had arrived in Spain she began to feel that there was a chance she might do well. By the time they finished their final workout in the gym on Friday afternoon there was a buzz of excitement spreading through the camp.

'Last week's competition was good,' said Kath. 'But I have a feeling that tomorrow will be even better. You can all relax in the morning, and then put on a real show for us in the evening.'

They were walking back to their rooms when they saw Danny and Courtney coming towards them, arm in arm. Danny smiled when he saw them, but Courtney's face looked pale and there were dark bags under her eyes.

'Hi, guys,' said Danny. 'I'm sorry I haven't been able to spend more time with you, but I've been kind of busy. We're looking forward to watching you all tomorrow night, though. Right, Courtney?'

Courtney smiled at them and Maxine realized that her gaze kept flickering to their feet. 'How come you all have new trainers?' she asked suddenly.

'We give them shoes whenever they need them,' Danny said, laughing. 'Didn't you know? That's the cool thing about being sponsored by Galactic. I see you're wearing the "Danny Crowe" edition, John!'

Danny Crowe was the public face of Galactic Sportswear. He appeared in all their TV ads and always wore their gear. The 'Danny Crowe' running shoes were the most expensive in their range, and John been thrilled when his coach had handed him the box.

'They're the best shoes ever,' he said.

'Maybe not,' said Danny, conspiratorially touching his nose. 'You wait and see.'

Danny and Courtney moved off down the path, Courtney clinging to Danny's arm. She seemed to be asking him a lot of questions.

'Weird,' said John. 'Do you remember? She asked us about shoes before.'

'She probably wants a job modelling them,'

Maxine said. 'But I can't imagine her wearing trainers. She'd be about ten centimetres shorter!'

Maxine and Jade were warming up together on Saturday evening when they saw Kerry Jones arriving at the track with Michael, Isabel and Danny. Several press photographers were with them, along with a small TV crew.

'I'm surprised Courtney isn't there,' Jade said. 'She likes having her photo taken.'

'She probably knew they wouldn't be interested in her,' Maxine said. 'Not with Kerry Jones there.'

Kerry Jones was a striking figure, even from a distance. Not only was she one of the finest athletes in the word, she was beautiful too, with huge, almond-shaped eyes and high cheekbones, her dark fringe cut at a sharp angle to fall across her face.

'You two!' exclaimed Kath. 'You should be

warming up! You'll have plenty of time to meet her later.' She bent over the bag she had left on a nearby bench, searching for something, then she patted the pockets of her tracksuit. 'Has anyone been in here?' she demanded.

'I'm not sure,' Maxine said. 'We weren't really watching.'

'Well, my locker key has gone,' Kath said grimly. 'I thought we'd put a stop to this nonsense. If I thought that you two . . . ? Come with me.'

Maxine glanced at Jade. This was awful. Kath couldn't really suspect *them*, could she? They followed her to the locker room. It was a scene that was becoming all too familiar. The door of Kath's locker hung open and the contents had clearly been disturbed.

Kath turned to them. 'Well?' she said.

'You can't think—' began Maxine, but Jade butted in, furious.

'We would never, *ever* do this,' she said. 'I can't believe you'd even ask us.'

Kath didn't speak, and Maxine saw that there were tears in her eyes. She wiped them away. 'This is ruining everything,' she said sadly. 'Of course I'll take your word. I'm sorry. But someone has done this, and every time something happens, you lot seem to be around. You can see why I'd—'

'No, I can't,' Jade said. 'You ought to trust us by now. Come on, Maxine. We've got a race to run.'

Maxine turned to Kath. 'Go on,' Kath said. 'She's right. Don't worry.'

Maxine returned to the warm-up area and tried to concentrate on her routine, but she felt shaken. Everything had been going so well, and now this. Long before she felt ready, she heard Jerry calling to her that the race was about to start. Looking at Jade she saw that she was still very angry about what had happened; the expression on her face told her that it was probably best not to try to speak to her right now.

They took their places on the track and Maxine found that she had been drawn in the outside lane. She touched Joshua's bracelet, hoping it would bring her luck. As she waited for the starter to call them to their marks, she heard Danny's voice: 'Go for it, Maxine!'

She glanced up and saw him standing with Kerry Jones. Kerry gave her a little wave, and Maxine was suddenly overcome with nerves. Michael and Isabel were also standing nearby and she was about to look away when she saw Courtney arrive, looking daggers at Kerry Jones. She stood beside Danny and thrust her arm through his as if she owned him. Courtney really was annoying. Maybe . . .

'To your marks!'

Maxine stepped forward and crouched, her heart suddenly pounding. The starting pistol cracked but she was slow to get away, and she knew at once that she had lost at least a metre on the others. She should have ignored what was going on beside the track. She was a fool!

Panic set in. She couldn't afford to let the others run away from her. She accelerated, sprinting as hard as she dared round the bend, and when she reached the mark on the track she cut across the other lanes at speed. As she reached the inside lane she saw that she had overdone it; she had run the bend far too fast and now she was a clear two metres ahead of the field.

She decided there was only one thing she could do now – she would run the whole race from the front. She had done it before, but never against opposition of this quality. As she pounded down the back straight and round the second bend she was uncomfortably aware of Hiari and Jade just a few short metres behind her, and she didn't have to look round to know that Hiari was running with her usual smooth, easy style.

As she came into the home straight for the first time she risked a glance back, and saw that her burst at the beginning had really stretched the field. Only two athletes were within striking distance: Hiari and Jade.

Nothing changed as she ran the bend, but as she continued down the back straight she could already feel the strain. Her breathing was coming harder and she could feel the tension growing in her shoulders. The final bend was approaching and there were only 200 metres left to run. At any moment she knew that Hiari and Jade would strike. She forced herself onward, hoping desperately that when the time came she would have the strength to respond. *But you won't*, said a voice in her head. *You set off too fast, and you know it. Your legs are going to give up on you.*

The finish line was coming closer all the time and still Maxine was in the lead. She was almost starting to believe she would do it when first Hiari, then Jade flashed past her. She saw the briefest flash of Jade's face, but it was enough to tell her that her friend was still fuelled by anger. From somewhere Jade managed to find another burst of speed and she overhauled Hiari in the last ten metres and won the race before collapsing, doubled up, on the ground.

Maxine shook hands with the other girls, trying to hide her disappointment. She was genuinely pleased for Jade, because beating Hiari was a magnificent achievement, but inside she was annoyed with herself. She knew that to win she needed total concentration, and she had allowed herself to be distracted.

And she had tensed up again. She had to stop herself doing that.

As the others walked off, Danny approached her. 'Great race,' he said. 'You were close, Maxine. Very close.'

Maxine shook her head. 'You know I wasn't,' she said. 'I was never going to win. Not after the start I had.'

'Don't be too hard on yourself,' replied Danny. 'Come and meet Kerry. She wants to talk to you.'

'Me?' said Maxine, her heart beating faster. 'Why?'

Danny picked up her bag. 'Don't worry,' he said. 'Come on.'

Maxine followed him over to where Kerry was waiting with Michael and Isabel.

'Hi, Maxine,' the champion said, shaking hands. 'It's good to meet you. Danny has been telling me all about you, haven't you, D?'

Kerry turned towards Danny, but Danny could do no more than raise a hand weakly in farewell as Courtney took him by the arm, whispered something in his ear and marched him away up the path, leaving Maxine, Kerry, Michael and Isabel all staring after him.

CHAPTER TEN

'What was all that about?' asked Kerry of nobody in particular as they watched Danny and Courtney disappear from view.

'That girl is a nightmare,' Isabel said, then clapped a hand over her mouth and blushed furiously as she realized that Maxine was staring at her.

'Don't worry,' said Michael. 'I don't think you've revealed any great secrets. Let's leave

Kerry to have a talk with Maxine. That's what Danny was planning.'

What had Danny been saying about her? Maxine wondered. She didn't dare ask. Kerry Jones was her idol — she had watched every race she had run this year on TV — and it was hard to believe that she was standing here talking to her.

'Don't look so worried,' Kerry said. 'Danny thought maybe I could help you, that's all. He said when he saw you last year you were one of the best young athletes he'd ever seen, but it's not been going so well lately.'

'You saw the race,' Maxine replied gloomily. 'I made all the wrong decisions, and I got the start wrong. I wasn't concentrating.'

'Well, there you go! You know what went wrong in that race, so you're halfway there. You only have light training tomorrow after the competition, right? So how about we go for a run together in the morning? Just you and me? Kath showed me some beautiful trails through the hills. We'll go early – five-thirty, say? I'll meet you here.'

When Kerry had gone Maxine collected her things and went to meet her friends. They were all eager to hear what Kerry had said to her, but Maxine suddenly felt embarrassed and couldn't bring herself to tell them that she and Kerry were going running together in the morning. It didn't seem right. Jade and Hiari were both better runners than she was. Jade's performance today had been awesome, and Hiari had been really generous in defeat. She was still telling Jade how well she had run. After a while Maxine told the others she was tired and went to her room, where she found a text on her phone from, Joshua:

Did you win?

No, thought Maxine, glancing down at her

bracelet. Then she wrote: **Nearly!** And added: **I met Kerry Jones!** Joshua had become as fanatical as she was about watching races, and he loved Kerry Jones. He'd be very excited.

Maxine set her alarm for five o'clock and tried to go to sleep. At first she kept re-running the evening's race in her head, seeing the others come past her so close to the end. If she could have just held out . . . But she knew that she'd lost the race at the start, not at the finish. Only that wasn't what Kerry had wanted to tell her . . .

Her thoughts drifted and the last thought she had before she fell asleep was a surprising one. It was the image of Courtney's face in the fiesta crowd last week, pale and scared as the man pointed angrily at her.

The alarm woke her with a start and for a moment she couldn't remember why she was awake so early. Then it all came back to her and she leaped out of bed and dressed quickly in her running gear, slipping Joshua's bracelet onto her wrist. It was dark outside, but when she went to the window she saw pale light growing in the sky away to the east. She slipped quietly out through the deserted corridors and into the scented darkness.

By the time she reached the running track the light in the eastern sky had grown strong enough to show Kerry doing some stretches on the grass.

She looked up and smiled when she saw Maxine approaching. 'Cool! You made it. I love running at this time of day.'

Maxine went carefully through her usual warm-up routine and then she and Kerry jogged down to the gates, which were closed. Kerry rattled them. 'You have to get Juan to open them,' Maxine said.

'I didn't realize. I mean, it's like a prison.'

'Things have been happening,' Maxine said.

'Security's very tight. Didn't you tell Michael we were going out?'

'No. I thought it would be our secret. There must be someone in the gatehouse, right?'

'Juan. He's probably asleep.'

Kerry went over and knocked on the window. A bleary-eyed Juan rose up out of the darkness and rubbed his eyes when he saw Kerry and Maxine standing there. 'No one comes in after dark without a pass,' he said.

'We're not coming in,' Kerry pointed out. 'We're going out. And when we come back it will be light, OK?'

Juan considered this for a few moments and then pressed a button and the gates swung open. As they set off up the mountain trail Maxine told Kerry about the strange happenings at Camp Gold.

'So you think one of you is making all this trouble?' Kerry asked.

'I hope not,' Maxine said. 'Michael seems to think it's someone coming in from outside, but none of us can think why anyone would. Nothing's been taken, but it's creepy thinking of someone going through our bags and lockers.'

'Well, let's forget about it for a while,' Kerry said. 'Let's see if we can be up on that hilltop at sunrise. That would be cool, right?'

The hilltop was several kilometres away, a jagged black outline against the sky. Soon they were running through woods over springy pine needles and Kerry began to tell Maxine about how she had discovered she could run.

'I was twelve years old,' she said, 'and I'd been at secondary school for a year when a new sports teacher came to the school, Mr Carter. He made everyone run. We did cross-country all through that winter and we had charts in the changing rooms to show how many kilometres we'd run. You could run at lunch times and after school too. I loved it. I won several big cross-country races that year, and when the summer came I made the county team for eight hundred metres and went to the national championships.

'That was when it started to get tough. I joined a club and I started training in the evenings. All I wanted to do was run, but my parents always wanted me to be a doctor and there was all that work to do for school, and my friends were always on at me to go shopping or go to a movie, or just hang out. I couldn't keep up.'

They were out of the trees now, jogging comfortably side by side along the dusty trail as the sky brightened even more. The only sounds were the crunch of their footsteps and the twitter of birds in the undergrowth.

'So what did you do?' asked Maxine curiously. Kerry's experiences sounded uncannily like her own.

'I knew what I wanted to do,' Kerry said. 'I wanted to run. I figured if my friends couldn't handle me having to work and do my training then they weren't worth it. I'm not saying it was easy, but when they said mean things to me just because I didn't want to go and hang out in the shopping mall on a Saturday, I knew I was right. I went to college and got myself a degree in sports science too, and I'm proud of that. I'm guessing you've had a hard year, right?'

Maxine nodded agreement. 'It's like you said. Everyone wants me to do things and there isn't enough time.'

'It's a big change,' Kerry agreed. 'But you know what? I found plenty of new friends. Friends who understood what I was doing. And not all of my old friends gave up when I wouldn't hang out all the time. My best friend Shanice was at nursery school with me.'

'I've got a friend like that. She's called Kayle.

She's a gymnast.' Maxine smiled, thinking of Kayle. 'It's a shame she can't be here. She would have loved it.'

'Yeah, we're lucky to be here, right? It's a beautiful morning and the sun's about to come up. I'll race you to the top.' Kerry set off at once at a sprint.

'Hey!' called Maxine, laughing. 'That's not fair.'

She dashed after Kerry, completely forgetting that she was chasing the world's fastest 800-metre runner as they raced together up the trail and stopped, breathing hard as an amazing scene met their eyes.

They had reached the highest point on the line of crags that rose sharply from the hills below, and now they could see away over the hills to the sea beyond, and the vast orange ball of the sun was rising out of the water into a clear blue sky.

'I knew it,' said Kerry, turning to Maxine with

her eyes shining. 'I knew this would be a great spot. Last year I watched the sun rise over the Grand Canyon and this is nearly as good.'

'It's awesome,' said Maxine. 'I've never seen anything like it.' The sun rose a little higher as they watched, and the light made the coloured stones on her bracelet glow as if they were alive.

'I reckon you'll probably be seeing the sun rise all over the world by the time you're my age,' said Kerry. 'Come on, let's get back. I'm starting to feel hungry.'

It was funny, thought Maxine as they ran back; Kerry, and Danny too – they were both famous, both amazing, but they were just like anyone else when you got to know them.

In a surprisingly short time they came over a low rise and saw Camp Gold ahead of them. Maxine halted, for in the distance, maybe four hundred metres beyond Camp Gold, a sleek, shiny black car was parked by the roadside. It was hard to tell from this distance, but it certainly looked like the same one she had seen before. It was the shininess that was so distinctive, as if its owner washed and polished it every night.

'Hey, come on,' called Kerry, pausing and looking back. 'I told you, I'm starving.'

Maxine gave a final glance at the car before setting off in pursuit. They dipped down through the woods, and when they came out on the road near Camp Gold, the car was out of sight. It was almost as though it had been deliberately parked there, thought Maxine, out of sight but still nearby.

They jogged in through the gates, waving to Juan as they passed, and on down to the track.

'How about we do a couple of fast laps?' asked Kerry. 'Just for fun.' Without waiting for an answer she was off round the track and Maxine followed without hesitation.

She felt good, as if the early-morning run had

given her energy. She surged after Kerry as she felt the pace accelerate and completed the two laps just a pace or two behind her.

'Guess what?' said Kerry as they jogged round the track one final time to warm down. 'That was as fast as you ran yesterday. A little faster, in fact,' she added, glancing down at the display on her watch.

'It can't have been.'

'It's true. You're as fast as any of those other girls. Faster, I reckon. Danny was right about you. It's in your blood. You just have to remember how it feels when it's all going right. Sure, you have to concentrate, but you have to let go too. Sometimes, when you want something real bad it's hard to relax, but that's what you have to do. Enjoy yourself!'

Kerry bent and picked up her bag, then walked off back up the path towards the entrance. Maxine sat down on a bench. She still couldn't quite believe that she had run so fast, and it had been effortless. She looked down at her wrist, remembering how Joshua's bracelet had glowed in the light of the rising sun. In future it would always remind her of exactly how good she had felt when running up on the hills with Kerry. She looked up when she heard footsteps behind her and she saw Jade, Hiari, Sasha and John.

'You are so lucky,' breathed Jade. 'I can't believe you didn't tell us.'

'Where did you go?' asked Sasha. 'I was awake and I heard your door. I saw you go out of Camp Gold but that was hours ago.'

'Not that long,' said Maxine. 'Only an hour. We went to watch the sunrise. It was awesome.'

'But what happened?' demanded John as they headed for the restaurant. 'Did she tell you things? Did she tell you about the Olympic finals?'

'She . . .' Maxine paused. 'Well, she told me about how hard it was when she was growing up. But mostly we just ran. It was awesome!'

She stopped. The others were no longer listening. They were staring towards the gates. Courtney was running up the drive. She turned onto the path and rushed past them.

'Did you see?' asked Sasha. 'She was crying!'

CHAPTER ELEVEN

The following day at training Maxine knew that something had changed. Even as she went through her warm-ups, she felt different. She couldn't tell whether it was the things Kerry had said to her, or the early-morning run and the incredible sunrise, or the fun game of basketball she and her friends had played during the afternoon, but it felt like she was starting again, and this time she was going to get it right.

There was another thing too, she thought, as she walked over to the track. They had been eating breakfast the previous day when they'd seen Danny and Courtney drive out of Camp Gold in their enormous hire car, and neither of them had returned since. Somehow Courtney's absence had made everyone feel more cheerful.

'Maybe Danny has gone to put her on an aeroplane,' said Sasha. 'Maybe she will never come back, and Danny will be fun again.'

'That would be great,' agreed John. 'Danny really helped me last year. This time he's hardly done any coaching. And we haven't seen him on the basketball court either.'

At breakfast this morning neither Danny nor Courtney had appeared, and Maxine was starting to think that the two of them wouldn't return. Like John, she would miss Danny. They all would. But it was probably for the best. Maybe they would all be able to concentrate better on their training too if they weren't also trying to keep an eye on Courtney.

'OK,' said Kath. 'We're going to do some more work on tempo this morning. I want you in two teams and you'll start on opposite sides of the track. You start on my whistle and you're going to run two hundred metres in forty seconds to start with. The cones by the side of the track are fifty metres apart and I'll give you a whistle every ten seconds. You should cross over exactly halfway round.'

Jerry, Hiari and Hui Zhong were all in Maxine's team, and as usual she found herself running with Hiari.

'You are not complaining about the heat today,' observed Hiari as they completed their first 200 metres exactly on time and passed the other group, led by Jade, going in the opposite direction.

'I know,' said Maxine. 'I think I might be

getting used to it. This is fun, but I wish we could go faster.'

'I think you're going to wish you hadn't said that,' laughed Hiari as Kath called a short break and then set them off at a pace that left them with no breath for talking.

When the end of the session approached Kath told them she wanted them to run time trials in pairs. 'We'll aim for some new personal bests today,' she said. 'It's a lot cooler this morning, and you're all rested. Let's see what we can do.' She paused. 'We have a special reason for needing your best performance today,' she continued. 'You remember that we told you our sponsors wanted us to trial these revolutionary new running shoes for them – the Meganovas? Well, they'll be arriving tomorrow.'

There was a burst of excited conversation. Kath held up a hand for silence.

'Michael will tell you more later, but the

scientists from Galactic Sportswear have asked us to get an up-to-date time for all of you today.'

The first pair to run was Jade and Hui Zhong. The other athletes looked on with interest as they completed the first lap at a blistering pace.

'They'll never keep it up,' said Maxine.

She was wrong. The two girls pushed each other right to the limit, but in the final thirty metres Jade found an extra burst of speed that carried her into a clear lead, and Hui Zhong couldn't respond.

'Jade gets better every time she runs,' said Hiari. 'She is like steel. Very tough.'

Maxine laughed. Jade was the exact opposite of Hiari. Hiari ran as if she was a wild animal, as if she was born running, but Jade seemed to fight against the track, forcing herself forwards. Kath called out the times. Jade clenched her fists as she heard that she had improved her PB by four tenths of a second. Hui Zhong had improved hers by a tenth. As they watched the other pairs race Maxine was surprised to find that she didn't feel nervous at all. Instead, she found herself remembering her night-time run with Hiari, and when she looked at the bracelet on her wrist, her dawn run with Kerry came back to her vividly. She knew what she had to do: she had to carry that feeling with her onto the track.

Kath called her forward and she stood beside Hiari, briefly touching her bracelet for luck. Kath's whistle blew and they took off, Hiari running in front, flowing over the ground as easily as water. Maxine followed like a shadow, matching her stride for stride. They were going fast. The tempo training was really working, she realized. It was as if she had a clock ticking inside her, and she knew that they were running faster than she had ever run before.

A very small voice somewhere in the back of her mind tried to warn her that this was too fast;

she could never keep it up. But she didn't care. She felt good. As they completed the first lap Kath called out the time and Maxine knew that, at last, she was going to improve her PB. Hiari was pushing on now, raising the pace, but Maxine stuck with her effortlessly. As they entered the final bend Hiari glanced over her shoulder and Maxine knew then that she was worried.

They came off the bend and into the final straight, and Maxine moved out, still running on Hiari's shoulder. With fifty metres to go, she accelerated. She moved into the lead, but only for a second. Hiari responded instantly and for several strides the two girls were running neck and neck. And then, from somewhere deep inside her, Maxine found an extra gear, a sudden burst of acceleration that left Hiari two paces behind her as she crossed the line.

There was a burst of applause from the other

runners, and when Maxine had recovered enough to look around she realized that everyone had stopped what they were doing to watch.

Kath was smiling at her. 'That's the fastest time that anyone has run so far,' she said. 'You're a tenth faster than Hiari – and she's taken a tenth off her PB! Well done, Maxine, you've taken nearly a second off your PB! Well done, everybody. I reckon you're all ready for the Olympic Stadium. It's going to be a terrific race.'

As they packed up their things Maxine saw Jade looking at her curiously. 'You found it again,' her friend said.

'What?'

'I don't know,' replied Jade. 'Whatever it was you had last year. And when you beat me at the Indoor Championships. You even look different, but I'm not sure how exactly.'

Maxine laughed. 'You're right. I can't believe I

just did that! Nearly a second off my PB! I feel different too. At least, I did, until Kath reminded us about the Olympic Stadium. We can't all win, can we? And we have to run in front of all those people.'

'I guess maybe we're all going to be running against each other for years,' Jade said. 'We'll probably all win some. But I would like to carry the Olympic torch. That would really be something and it would make my grandma so happy. She's so old she lives in a residential home now, but she always wants to know everything I do.'

It would be the same for all of them, Maxine thought as they walked back to the locker room. All of them must have families and friends who would be so happy to see them carry the torch.

And only one of them could succeed.

It had been a good morning. As the athletes gathered for lunch Maxine could sense that the whole atmosphere at Camp Gold International had changed. Michael and Isabel joined the students in the restaurant, chatting easily as they moved among the tables. They had already heard about Maxine's new PB.

'It looks like your eight-hundred-metres race is going to be one of the hottest things in the competition,' Michael said.

'I don't know,' said Isabel. 'The pole-vault looks pretty good to me. There's nothing to choose between Sasha and Diane.'

'Except that I will win this time,' said Sasha.

'I don't think so,' said Diane, the tanned Australian girl, from a nearby table.

Isabel laughed. 'That's why I'm looking forward to it,' she said. 'And don't worry, John. We haven't forgotten about you.'

John looked up from his chicken and rice. 'When's Danny going to be back?' he asked. 'He said he was going to give us some help, but we haven't seen him at all this week.'

Michael and Isabel looked at each other. 'He's been very busy,' Isabel said finally. 'But he'll be back this afternoon. I'm sure he'll do his best for you, John. Oh . . . we have to go now.'

Michael was waving to someone on the other side of the restaurant. It was the tall man in the white suit they'd seen talking to Michael and Isabel the week before. He had a black laptop bag slung over his shoulder. The three of them took a secluded table at the edge of the terrace and were soon deep in conversation over the laptop.

'What's all that about?' said John.

'I'm not sure,' said Maxine, 'but they look excited, don't they? It has to be something good.'

Maxine was woken the next morning by the sound of raised voices. Shortly afterwards she heard footsteps on the stairs and there was a knock on her door: 'Everyone up, please, and in the lecture theatre in fifteen minutes.'

Maxine dressed quickly and joined the steady stream of students making their way downstairs. Michael was standing outside the entrance to the lecture theatre saying something angrily to Kath, who turned away and ran towards the gym complex. He hardly seemed to see the students as they filed in through the door. When they had all arrived he marched down to the front and stood looking up at the banked rows of worried faces.

'We've had a break-in,' he said. 'Another one. Last night several of the offices were ransacked and someone tried to access the computer network. In the process they erased a huge amount of information about your performances, and as far as I can see they achieved very little else. There's no sign of anyone coming onto the site over the fence, so it has to be somebody on the inside. That's why you are here now. I don't want to believe that any of you are involved, but one of you must know something about this. Didn't anyone notice anything odd last night?'

There was a very long, awkward silence. No one said anything.

'This can't happen again,' said Michael finally. 'It just can't, and we're going to make sure that it doesn't. We have a security firm coming in to fix up a CCTV system as soon as possible. From now on we'll be monitoring every part of this site, day and night. We can't afford for anything else to happen because we're starting the footwear trial for Galactic shortly, which I believe your individual coaches have told you about already. And they've already stressed how important it is to keep this under wraps – we're trusting you all here, so don't let us down. The shoes are called Meganova and if they're as good as Galactic say they are, you'll be breaking records in them before long. But you're to treat them like gold dust. They'll be checked out to you each time you use them, and checked back in afterwards. And you're to tell no one about the trials. Is that totally understood?'

There was a murmur of agreement. John raised a hand. 'What's so special about these shoes?' he asked.

'You've probably all heard of the new swimsuits they introduced a few years back,' Michael said. 'They helped swimmers to go faster. A lot of new world records were set with them. These shoes can do the same thing. If you think about it, you can run faster in trainers than you can in wellington boots. These shoes will make your existing trainers feel like wellington boots. But if word gets out to the press, or worse, if Galactic's competitors get their hands on the shoes, then we'll be looking for new sponsors for Camp Gold International.'

Maxine was only half listening to what Michael was saying as she was remembering something that had had happened on their very first morning. She could hear Courtney's voice now: *Do you need a lot of special equipment . . . ? Your shoes . . . they must be special ones . . .*

Suddenly everything fell into place. It had made no sense for Courtney to be playing stupid pranks, but if she was looking for something . . . something she couldn't find because it wasn't there . . . and that man she'd been meeting . . . maybe she was working for him . . ..

But it was no good.

It didn't fit, after all, because Courtney wasn't even there any more.

CHAPTER TWELVE

'Why are you looking like that, Maxine?' asked
Sasha as they walked outside.

'It's nothing. I had an idea, but I was
wrong.'

'You might as well tell us,' John said.

'I was thinking about Courtney,' said Maxine
uncertainly. 'About the things she said right at
the beginning when she was asking us about our
trainers. Remember?'

'That's right,' said Sasha. 'She was very annoying.'

'She asked again a few days ago,' said John thoughtfully.

'I just thought, she might have been trying to find out about these new running shoes. Only then I remembered that she wasn't even here last night, so it couldn't have been her who—'

'But it could!' exclaimed Sasha. 'Last night I could not sleep. I was having a dream.' She paused, frowning. 'I was in the Olympic Stadium, in the pole-vault. My pole kept breaking. It was very bad—'

'Sasha!' said Maxine. 'We were talking about Courtney, remember.'

'It was a very bad dream,' Sasha said. 'I woke up and that is when I heard the car. It was the middle of the night. I went to my window and it was Danny and Courtney.'

'So she *was* here,' Maxine said. 'She could have

done it. You see, I was thinking about that man we saw her with. What if he was from one of the other sportswear companies? What if Courtney is actually some kind of a spy?'

There was a pause. Then John nodded slowly. 'It does kind of make sense,' he said. 'And you remember where we found your bracelet, Maxine? It was right outside Danny's office. Maybe Courtney picked it up by accident when she was going through your bag.'

'That bracelet does catch on things,' Maxine said. 'And of course if she was looking for special running shoes that's why she didn't take anything.'

'We have to tell Michael,' said Jade, who had been listening quietly. 'You heard what he said. If someone steals these shoes when they arrive, it could be the end of Camp Gold.'

'But I don't think we can,' said John. 'We haven't actually got any proof that it was her, have we? We'd look kind of stupid if she can prove she couldn't have done any of those things.'

'What about that man?' demanded Sasha. 'There was something wrong about that. He was a bad man. It is obvious.'

'Why don't we just keep watch,' suggested John, 'like you wanted to before, Sasha, when you thought she was two-timing Danny? If she really is after these shoes then she's bound to try to get at them.'

'I don't think it's going to be easy for anyone to steal them,' Maxine said. 'I bet they'll be locked up all the time we're not actually wearing them.'

While they were talking, a dark blue security van turned in at the gates.

'That must be the shoes!' exclaimed Sasha. 'It has to be.'

The van drew up outside the main entrance

and Michael and Isabel came outside as a car arrived driven by the tall, white-suited man. He spoke briefly to Michael and then the van drove along the side of the gym block and stopped beside the door of a storeroom, which Michael unlocked.

The security guards unloaded a series of boxes, watched by Michael and the stranger. Michael locked the door and the van drove off.

'They'll keep them there every night, I expect,' John said. 'That man must be from Galactic. We could watch from the trees over there. If we take it in turns we can watch all night.'

'And if we get caught they'll send us home,' Maxine said. 'Michael won't give us any more chances. You know he won't.'

'If the shoes are stolen there won't even *be* a Camp Gold,' Sasha said. 'We *have* to watch.'

The first trials of the new shoes were to be

held that evening. Maxine spent the morning in the gym, and the afternoon in the pool. There was no sign of Courtney or Danny. Late in the afternoon Maxine, Jade, Sasha and Hiari were making their way back to their rooms when two more vans arrived, bearing the logo of the security firm who had delivered the shoes. From the first van, two men emerged, straightening their caps. Michael appeared, with Juan, the gatekeeper, beside him. Juan began to protest loudly and angrily, but Michael shook his head and the two uniformed security guards walked off towards the gate. Juan went back inside, muttering and making gestures with his hands.

'Looks like he might have lost part of his job,' Jade said.

Two men in suits had climbed out of the other van and Michael turned to speak to them. He indicated the eaves of the buildings, pointing to various locations.

'Cameras,' said Sasha. 'Maybe we will not need to watch after all.'

But the men were shaking their heads. One of them glanced at his watch and the other said 'Mañana' and opened the door of the van. Michael protested loudly, but both men shrugged and moments later they drove away.

'So much for the cameras,' said Maxine.

By the time the athletes arrived at the track that evening several more cars had arrived at Camp Gold, bringing with them a large group of scientists and executives from Galactic Sportswear. The executives sat beside the track with Michael and several of the coaches. Danny and Isabel were with them, and Maxine thought that Danny looked tired and fed up. Isabel was wearing dark glasses and her mouth was set in a thin line.

The athletes warmed up as usual, and then

they were called over to the group of scientists to be fitted with their new shoes. Maxine sat on a canvas stool and a young woman with stylish narrow-framed spectacles selected a box from the stack behind her. 'My name's Helen,' she said, taking a gold-and-white running shoe from the box.

'What's so special about them?' asked Maxine as Helen felt carefully around her foot before rejecting the shoe and selecting another one.

'Well, I guess you've been running long enough to know how important it is to choose the right shoes for the shape of your feet and the way you run?'

Maxine nodded. She remembered being surprised about how careful her coach had been to fit her with the right shoes the year before. Until then she'd thought that all running shoes were more or less the same.

'And you know that you need to get the

maximum energy each time your foot is in contact with the ground? That's what these shoes are designed to do. You could say that they're intelligent shoes. The soles are made of a revolutionary compound that reacts to the way you move and shapes itself to give you the best possible support. As for how it works, well, that's still top-secret. I'm not allowed to tell you. There, how does that feel? Stand up and walk around.'

'Wow!' Maxine felt as if she was walking on air. And there was a tingling sensation in the muscles of her calves. It was incredible. She could hear the startled exclamations of the other athletes all around her. 'These feel awesome!' she said, jogging around in a little circle. 'I can't wait to get on the track.'

She didn't have long to wait. When all the athletes were ready they began a regular training session. 'This feels so different,' said Maxine as the distance runners jogged between sprints. 'It feels like my legs are recovering much quicker than normal.'

Beside her, Jade agreed.

'It's like running with no shoes on,' added Hiari. 'Only better!'

But it was when the runners began a series of time trials that the real power of the shoes became clear. Every 100-metre runner produced a personal best, and it was the same story with the 400 metres. John had a huge smile on his face as he told them he'd bettered his previous time by a tenth of a second.

'It might not be the shoes, though,' Jade said doubtfully. 'It might just be that everyone's excited.'

'We know that,' said Helen, who was standing nearby. 'We'll be doing a lot more tests today and tomorrow, but so far what we're seeing seems pretty much in line with what we were finding back in the States. I guess you guys are up next. Good luck!'

Maxine ran with the first group. Running in the new shoes was pure enjoyment, and as they came up to complete the first lap she felt unbelievably relaxed. Beside her, Hui Zhong was smiling as she ran. Hui Zhong never smiled when she was running, but then Maxine saw that there were smiles on the faces of the other runners too. And as Kath looked up from her stopwatch Maxine saw the excitement in her eyes. They must be going very fast indeed!

Maxine pushed herself harder, and somewhere on the back straight she dropped Hui Zhong. She continued to accelerate and ran the final 100 metres at a flat-out sprint. She slowed to a jog when she had crossed the line. Her muscles still felt relaxed, although she was breathing hard. She turned and walked back to Kath.

'That's another PB,' Kath said. 'A tenth of a second faster!'

'Just like John,' Maxine said.

'Just like most people.' Kath smiled. 'And now you'd better get those shoes off.' She gestured with her head to where Helen was waiting. 'They'll take you inside and do one or two tests, then you're done for the day.'

'They're like magic shoes from a fairy tale,' Maxine said as Helen removed them from her feet and put them away in a carefully labelled box. 'Do we get to keep them when this is over?'

Helen shook her head. 'We have at least two more months' work to do before they can go into production. And until they go on sale we have to make sure no one finds out what we're up to. These shoes could revolutionize running.'

'But I thought we'd be able to wear them in the Olympic Stadium,' said Maxine.

'I'm afraid not. We can't let anyone see these

in public until we're absolutely sure they're right. Sorry.'

The team from Galactic Sportswear were not taking any chances with the shoes. Each pair was carefully boxed and ticked off on a list on a computer, then all the boxes were returned to the storeroom. Maxine and her friends watched from a distance as Michael locked the door, checked the handle and then walked away, following the very satisfied group of scientists and Galactic VIPs to the restaurant.

'He's just left it!' exclaimed Sasha. 'He is crazy.'

'Well, it *is* locked,' John pointed out. 'And it looks like a serious lock. Let's go get some food. Running that fast has given me an appetite.'

'We cannot all eat at the same time,' declared Sasha. 'Someone must stay here.'

John sighed. 'Don't worry,' he said. 'You guys go on ahead. Just don't be too long, OK?'

'I'll wait with you,' said Maxine. 'I'm still too

excited to eat. Can you believe those shoes?'

She and John were so busy discussing the possibilities of the new footwear that the time passed quickly. No one came near the storeroom door, but Maxine did wonder briefly why Michael hadn't hired a security guard to watch over it. When the others returned it was dark, and the sky was full of stars, but they could still see the door clearly, illuminated by the small spotlights that were set into all the pavements at Camp Gold International.

Maxine and John ate quickly and returned stealthily to the shelter of the trees. Maxine was relieved to find that, even quite close to, she couldn't see the watchers hidden in the shadows.

'Has anything happened?' she whispered.

'No,' replied Jade softly. 'We don't all need to stay here. Why don't we take turns?'

But they were all far too excited to go to bed.

'Let's stay until one o'clock,' said Maxine. 'We can take it in turns after that.'

They all agreed. Ten o'clock came and went. Another half-hour passed and lights began to go out in the residential areas. An owl hooted – a real one this time. They looked at each other and smiled.

Then they heard footsteps on the path, but it was only Juan. He paused by the door, rattled the handle, grunted something in Spanish under his breath and moved on, shining his torch into the dark areas between the buildings as he went.

More lights went out. Gradually, as time passed, Camp Gold fell silent. Midnight came and went, and they heard the sounds of voices, men and women calling goodnight to each other. Maxine heard Kath laughing about something. Then silence fell.

And then, just when they had all stopped expecting anything to happen, a hooded figure appeared on the path and made its way towards the door. They heard the faint jingle of keys and a muffled curse, then the hood was thrown back impatiently and they saw Courtney, struggling to fit a key into the lock.

CHAPTER THIRTEEN

'I knew it!' hissed Sasha. 'I knew it all the time.'

'Quiet,' hissed John. 'We have to surround her, so she can't get away. Jade, Hiari, you go round to the left. Sasha and Maxine, go right. We'll all arrive together in thirty seconds' time, OK? Go!'

Maxine wanted to stop them. She knew they ought to fetch Michael or one of the other adults, but Sasha was already moving and Jade and Hiari had disappeared into the shadows.

'Hurry, Maxine,' John whispered.

There was no time to argue. Maxine slipped away behind Sasha. They moved quickly round behind some low bushes and edged along the wall of the building. Courtney was still fumbling with the keys when John came up behind her.

'What are you doing?' he asked.

Courtney jumped and gave a strangled yell of fear and surprise. The keys fell jangling to the ground. She flattened herself back against the wall, her eyes wide with panic as she saw the five figures surrounding her. Then her eyes seemed to come into focus. 'But . . . you're just kids,' she said. 'I've seen you on the track.'

'I asked you what you were doing,' repeated John. 'No one's allowed in there.'

'Well, *I* am,' said Courtney, suddenly more confident. 'Obviously I am. I have the keys.' She bent down and picked them up. 'I was just going to . . . I was going to . . .'

'One of us should fetch Michael,' John said.

'I'll go,' said Maxine, relieved that they were finally doing the right thing. But before she had taken two steps she heard Courtney's voice.

'Stop! Wait!'

'Ignore her,' Sasha said. 'She is a bad woman. She was going to destroy everything.'

'No, listen,' said Courtney. 'Please listen. You don't understand. I . . . didn't want to do it. They said if I didn't . . . they said I'd never work again.' She was sobbing now, taking in big gulps of air. The words came out in bursts. 'I was stupid. I know I was. They said I had to get them the shoes. But I'm not going to. Not now. Please don't tell Michael. Please.'

'This is nonsense!' exclaimed Sasha contemptuously. 'Go on, Maxine. Bring Michael.'

'No, wait,' said John. 'I don't understand. Who told you to steal the shoes?'

'Flame,' said Courtney, naming the world's

third biggest sportswear company. 'I had just landed the job modelling their swimwear and they found out I was going out with Danny . . .'

'That was not hard,' commented Sasha. 'You made sure it was in all the papers.'

'It's my job,' said Courtney with a sudden show of defiance. 'I have to keep up my public profile.'

Sasha snorted.

'Modelling for Flame was my big break,' Courtney continued, 'but they'd heard about these new shoes that Galactic were making and they said, why didn't I come to Camp Gold with Danny and see if I could get hold of a pair for them? They said I would get lots more jobs if I did, and I couldn't see what harm it would do. It was only a pair of shoes.'

'That's not what you said before,' Jade commented. 'You said they threatened you.'

'That was after I'd got here,' Courtney replied.

'They sent someone to put pressure on me. He said if I didn't get the shoes he had contacts in the modelling business and they'd make sure I'd never get another job . . . Look, I made a mistake, OK? They made me do this. I hate them all. Please don't tell anyone you found me here. I can quit modelling. I'll leave here and go back to college. I want to be with Danny. That's all I ever wanted. You mustn't say anything. There's no harm done, is there?' Courtney burst into loud sobs.

'I don't believe a word of that,' said Maxine disgustedly.

'Me neither,' said a voice. Two tall figures detached themselves from the shadow of a doorway further along the wall. Michael and Danny walked purposefully towards them. Courtney took one look at them and collapsed. John just managed to catch her and lower her gently to the ground and they all stood there for a moment, looking down at her.

'Shouldn't we . . . do something?' said Maxine.

'She'll be fine,' Danny said harshly. 'She's a very good actress. I doubt if she's really fainted.'

'All the same,' said Michael, crouching beside her. 'I think I'll just make sure. No, she's fine.'

Courtney gave a groan and he told her to lie still for a moment. He took off his jacket and placed it under her head.

'I don't know why you're doing that,' Danny said bitterly. 'She deserves to suffer. She made a fool out of me.'

'She fooled all of us,' Michael said. 'She made out she was stupid, but I don't think she is.'

'Right,' agreed Danny. 'I think she was working for them before we ever got together. I think they planned the whole thing.'

'The only problem was, we didn't have the shoes here.'

'She met a man in town,' Maxine said. 'We

saw them. He was shouting at her.'

'Why didn't you say?' demanded Danny, turning towards her. 'You could have saved us a whole lot of trouble.'

'We thought maybe they were, you know . . . we thought maybe he was a boyfriend,' Sasha said. 'We did not like her, but it was not our business.'

'Oh,' said Danny, looking embarrassed. 'Yeah, well, like I say, I was a fool. But not any more.'

'But, you were waiting for her,' Maxine said.

'Too right,' replied Michael grimly. 'You thought we'd leave this place unguarded? I tried to get the cameras fitted, but they couldn't do it until the morning.'

'We saw,' said Jade.

'Did you now?' Michael looked curiously at them. 'You've been acting as unpaid private detectives, have you? Keeping a watch on everyone?'

'N–n–no,' stammered Maxine. 'We just happened to be there.'

'And tonight? Don't tell me you were skulking in those trees by accident.'

'We were trying to help,' said John.

'You know how you can really help?' Michael said, and Maxine could see that he was very tired. 'You can work hard over the next few days and do your very best at the Olympic Stadium.'

'I'll be there at training tomorrow,' Danny said. 'From now on I won't miss a session. I wish I was running in the exhibition event in Barcelona too. They invited me, but I wasn't sure my hamstring would be better.'

'And now you should all get to bed,' Michael said. 'You've got an early start in the morning. But you're not to say a word about this. If the people from Galactic find out that we've had a serious security breach like this, well, they might just walk away anyway.'

'But nothing has happened,' said Maxine. 'Not really. I mean, she didn't manage to get the shoes.'

'All the same, I think we'll just say that Courtney and Danny had a big bust-up and leave it at that, OK?'

'Well, that's true at least,' said Danny grimly.

The next day Courtney had gone.

Everyone knew it; everyone was talking about it at breakfast.

Michael came into the restaurant while they were all eating and announced that there would be one final session of testing with the new shoes. 'After that you'll have two more days to prepare for the big event,' he said. 'Pay attention to your coaches and work hard. We agreed to trial these shoes as part of our sponsorship deal with Galactic and I know it's been a distraction. We'd hoped to get it over with in the first week, but the shoes weren't ready in time. Even so, I think it's been worth it to secure these fantastic training facilities for the next three years, and to pay for all of you to come here.'

There were some cheers as Michael said this, but he held up a hand for silence. 'There have been too many disturbances since we arrived here. Now you have to really focus. Believe me, it's no joke running in front of all those people. We wouldn't have agreed if we didn't think you were all good enough, but I'm afraid only some of you will be able to run on the day. Your coaches will select you during the next few days. Good luck to all of you.'

'I didn't realize,' Maxine said to Jade. 'I thought we'd all be running.'

'I guess there's only one race for each event. There are sixteen eight-hundred-metre runners so only half of us can go. Don't worry, you'll make it. Michael's right. Now we can concentrate on the running.' Jade sighed. 'I can't believe they won't let us run in the new shoes at the event – they felt so amazing yesterday. They definitely helped me to do a PB.'

'They're still top secret, though, aren't they?' Maxine replied. 'But if Galactic carry on sponsoring Camp Gold then I bet we'll be some of the first to wear them for real.'

'That would be so cool,' Jade agreed.

Their final session with the scientists from Galactic was short. The technicians collected video from all kinds of angles of the athletes running in their normal shoes and in the new ones.

'We'll be analysing the footage later,' Helen explained to Maxine. 'We'll be staying on here for the next few days to work on it. And maybe even have a bit of a holiday,' she added with a grin. 'I think they're going to let us come and watch you all run.'

'Some of us,' said Maxine. 'If we're selected.'

When the scientists had left the trackside, training began in earnest. Danny was true to his word and took part alongside the young athletes. His hamstring was obviously much better and he was just as focused as they were, as if he was trying to make up for lost time, and Maxine started to see the intensity that had made Danny into a top athlete. He led by example and training had a new edge to it with him around.

But even while she worked hard, Maxine found that she was able to remember Kerry Jones's advice and stay relaxed. She ran consistently fast times over the next few sessions, and no one was surprised when she was selected in the final group for the 800 metres.

Maxine was relieved and pleased to discover that her best friends had been chosen too, so they would all be travelling to Barcelona together the following day. But now that the event was so close, they were all nervous, and in the restaurant that evening they were finding it hard to eat the big bowls of pasta that were steaming in front of them.

'It is too quick,' said Sasha, looking unusually pale. 'I cannot believe that three weeks have gone so fast. I am not ready.'

'Sure, you are,' said John. 'You're more ready than any of us. And this time I bet you really will beat Diane.'

'I hope so,' Sasha replied. 'I want very much to carry the Olympic torch. I will go back to the village in Russia where I have many relations. They will be very proud. But first I must win.'

'You will,' Maxine said. 'You're always telling us to believe.'

'I know. But I keep having those bad dreams. Every time I run up, my pole breaks!'

There was a stir at the far side of the restaurant as Danny Crowe entered, with Kerry Jones by his side. The two of them collected some food from Rosalita, who was serving behind the counter, and made their way to a free table near where Maxine was sitting with her friends.

Kerry saw her and gave her a wave and a smile. 'How's it going?' she called over to them.

'We're all nervous,' Maxine replied, and when Kerry and Danny came to join them she told them about Sasha's dream.

'It is nothing,' said Sasha, embarrassed. 'I know that this will not happen.'

'Of course it won't,' laughed Kerry. 'But you know, I think you've all done as much training as you need. You should really take it easy before the big event. That's what I'm going to do. I've been working hard all week. I'm racing against Feluke Okoye tomorrow. She's the world record holder and I've only beaten her once.'

'Yeah, in the World Championships,' said Jade with a grin. 'The one that really counts.'

'Well, I don't want her to beat me tomorrow,' Kerry said. 'So I guess I'm a bit nervous too. Once we get into Barcelona, I'm going for a walk to take my mind off it. Hey! Maybe you could come. We could ask Michael.'

'I don't know,' said Danny. 'He wasn't too pleased when this lot went to the fiesta without asking.'

'He told you!' said Maxine. 'He said he wouldn't say anything.'

'I'm his best mate,' replied Danny.

'I'll talk to him,' Kerry said, and when she had finished eating she went in search of Michael. They returned together a short time later.

'Kerry's right,' Michael said to the group of friends, then he stood up and addressed the whole restaurant. 'You've all been working hard and a couple of hours' sightseeing in the afternoon will do no harm. You can go in groups, each group with two adults. Just make sure you're all at the stadium in plenty of time.'

There was a cheer from the assembled athletes. 'Me and Danny will come with you lot,' Kerry said to Maxine and her friends. 'Michael told us not to let you out of our sight.'

'I feel better,' said Sasha suddenly. 'I *will* win tomorrow. Of course I will win.'

But when Maxine came down for breakfast the following morning she saw that everyone was looking grim. She went over to join John and Hiari.

'There's been another break-in,' John said. 'It's the worst thing that could possibly have happened.'

'But the cameras,' said Maxine. 'The extra security . . .'

'I don't know how they did it,' John said. 'But the door of the storeroom was smashed and there's no doubt about it. Three boxes of shoes are missing.'

CHAPTER FOURTEEN

Maxine, Jade and Sasha were the first people
to arrive at the lecture theatre. Maxine saw
Michael sitting behind the desk, his shoulders
slumped and his head in his hands. Isabel
stood behind him with her hands on his
shoulders. He looked up as they came in,
rubbed his eyes, ran his hands through his hair
and got to his feet. He and Isabel stood and
watched as the students filed in silently. When

they were all assembled, he began to speak.

'This is a disaster for Camp Gold,' he told them. 'I've spoken to the chairman of Galactic Sportswear this morning. You've all seen him, I'm sure – the tall guy in the white suit. He's a very angry man, and I don't blame him. We did everything we could to keep these footwear trials a secret, but he's putting the blame on us. I very much doubt if they'll continue their sponsorship for another year.'

There were groans of disappointment.

'I know,' said Michael. 'This place was my dream and it's taken years of hard work to get it up and running. With the shoe trials and this incredible event today in the Olympic Stadium we thought we'd cracked it. We thought Camp Gold International would be bringing on young athletes for years to come. And now this.' He took a deep breath. 'This is what I want you to do,' he said. 'You might be the last group of athletes who ever have this opportunity, so I want you to go out there and make us all proud of you. Show the crowd, and all the people watching on TV, that with hard work and brilliant coaching it's possible to achieve your dreams.'

Someone began to clap, then more people joined in. Maxine looked along the row and began to applaud with her friends. John stood up, and soon everyone was on their feet, cheering, shouting and clapping.

'Thank you,' said Michael when the noise finally subsided. 'You're all wonderful. I know that many of you have already had to cope with the disappointment of not being selected to compete today, but I want you to remember that every person who came here to Camp Gold International will be going home with a new personal best to their name.'

There was more applause at this. Maxine

looked around the room. There were an awful lot of people who wouldn't be competing, and she knew how she would have felt if she'd been one of them.

'It's a hard fact about track and field,' Michael continued. 'There can only be one winner. We all keep going because we're determined that one day that winner might be us, right?' There was a loud chorus of agreement. 'OK . . .' 'Now, the police will be here soon and it's going to be no fun watching them poking around. I want you to do just what we planned. Get on the bus, go to Barcelona, spend the day sightseeing and shopping, and then show everyone what you can do tonight. I know you'll be awesome.'

By the time Maxine had collected her things and rejoined her friends in the entrance, several buses had pulled up outside and most of the athletics coaches were waiting there too. Danny and Kerry seemed to be in charge.

'Leave your kit here in the entrance,' Kerry said. 'It'll all be waiting for you when you arrive at the stadium later.'

They piled onto the buses in their groups. As they had said the night before, Danny and Kerry were coming with Maxine and her friends.

'They seem to be very friendly with each other,' Maxine whispered to Sasha, who was sitting next to her. 'You don't think . . .'

But before Sasha could tell her what she thought, Danny and Kerry sat down in the seat in front of them. Then, as the bus was going down the drive, they passed three police cars coming in at the gate. Maxine saw Danny staring gloomily at them through the window.

'This is all my fault,' he muttered to Kerry. 'If I hadn't brought Courtney here they'd never have—'

'They knew about the shoes already,' Kerry said. 'Don't beat yourself up about it.'

'I can't believe I was that stupid,' Danny said. 'These girls weren't fooled – were you, girls?'

Maxine blushed as Danny turned and looked back between the seats. He must have realized they were listening. 'I . . . we . . .' she stammered, before Sasha came to her rescue.

'How did they manage to break in?' she asked. 'There are cameras. There are men in uniforms. There is Juan!'

'Exactly,' said Danny. 'The security guards were patrolling and Juan was watching the cameras.'

'He fell asleep!' Maxine said.

'Right. This guy cut through the fence and broke down the door. You can see it all on the CCTV. If Juan had spotted it, we would have caught him red-handed. But he didn't.'

'Well, there's nothing we can do about any of that now,' said Kerry. 'Have any of you been to Barcelona before? No? You're going to love it. The best thing you can all do is perform brilliantly tonight, and if you're going to do that you mustn't spend the day worrying about Camp Gold.'

Before long the bus was driving though the suburbs of the great Catalan city. Eventually it pulled up in a street thronging with tourists. There were palm trees and pine trees, and above them all rose an extraordinary complex of towers and walls, all carved from stone, glittering with mosaics and crowned with golden flowers.

'It's the Sagrada Família,' Kerry told them as they climbed out into the dusty heat. 'The church of the Holy Family.'

'But they're still building it!' exclaimed Maxine. 'Look at the cranes.' High as the building was, skeletal yellow cranes towered above it.

'They've been building it for more than a hundred years,' Kerry said, checking that they were all there. 'This way. We can go up those towers. The view is amazing.'

'No way!' said Sasha. 'You said we were going to relax. We can't climb up there.'

'Don't worry,' Danny said, laughing. 'We go up in a lift. The hardest work you'll have to do is waiting in this heat.'

They joined a queue. It was long, but it moved surprisingly fast, and soon they were shooting up almost to the top of the highest towers. When they emerged onto a narrow walkway, the whole of Barcelona was spread out below them – from the glittering sea to the distant hills. Even more amazing were the carved towers.

'They're like trees!' exclaimed Maxine. 'They're covered with leaves.'

'And look,' said Jade. 'There are birds too. All carved out of stone.'

Every centimetre of every tower and wall was carved and ornamented with leaves and flowers and animals and people. As they edged along the dizzying walkways, gazing down at the ant–like people in the squares and streets far below, Maxine realized that Kerry had chosen this place very cleverly. It was the perfect way to take their minds off everything else. Only Sasha seemed a little subdued and strangely reluctant to look at the incredible views.

After they left the church they travelled on the metro to the Plaça de Catalunya and emerged into a seething mass of tourists. They turned into a side street, leaving the crowds behind. Before long they found a resaurant in a quiet square, where they sat outside and ate lunch.

'Thank you, Kerry,' said Sasha. 'It has been a very good day.'

'Right,' said John. 'I feel like I'm on vacation.'

'That's great,' said Kerry, looking at her watch. 'We just have time to walk down the Ramblas, and then I think we should start making our way to the stadium.'

They left the restaurant and Kerry led them through a narrow street. 'This is the Ramblas,' she told them as they emerged onto a broad avenue with a wide, tree-shaded pavement running right down the middle between two lanes of traffic. The central section was lined with stalls selling canaries in cages, brightly coloured scarves, pottery, newspapers – almost anything you wanted, it seemed to Maxine. And between the stalls there were buskers, street performers of every possible kind, including the most amazing human statues Maxine had ever seen. She was admiring a three-metre-high statue of Marie Antoinette (the person inside the costume was standing on a stool) when she suddenly caught sight of a familiar face.

The man was crossing the road with a bulky carrier bag in his hand, searching for a gap in the traffic, clearly in a hurry. He wore a smart suit and he looked like a businessman on his lunch break. But Maxine couldn't work out where she had seen him before.

And then the man stepped off the pavement into the path of a car. It didn't slow down. Its horn blared and the man jumped quickly back onto the pavement, snarling at the driver. As soon as his face twisted in anger Maxine knew him. When she had last seen that bald head, long nose and prominent jaw, the man had been snarling into Courtney's frightened face.

Maxine reached out and grabbed Jade's arm, pointing urgently. The others looked at her, then turned and saw the man crossing the road. He disappeared behind a stall for a moment, then emerged very close to them, moving quickly towards the opposite side of the Ramblas.

'Look,' said Maxine breathlessly. 'In the bag. There are boxes in there. It must be the shoes!'

'Why do you wait?' demanded Sasha as John

turned to look for Danny and Kerry. Maxine spotted them, but they were a a little way away, inspecting a junk stall with a large group of students. 'He is getting away,' said Sasha. 'I am going after him.'

'Sasha, wait . . .' called John.

But she was already gone, crossing the road and darting down a side street after the man. The others exchanged glances, and then set off after her in unspoken agreement.

They were lucky. The lights on the crossing turned green as they approached and they dashed across it, drawing some loud yells of disapproval from the tourists they jostled on their way.

'There!' said Hiari, pointing.

Sasha's unmistakable head of red hair bobbed along the crowded street ahead of them, then suddenly disappeared down a side turning. When they reached it they found themselves in a narrow alleyway between tall buildings. There was no one in sight, but they could hear footsteps echoing and they raced after them as the alleyway twisted and turned. It was shady here and amazingly quiet. It was hard to believe that the bustling streets were so close by.

They turned a corner and saw Sasha. She was standing at the entrance to a small square, looking around, confused. On the far side of the square a small group of skateboarders sat on a bench while one of them attempted to jump down a flight of steps.

'He is gone,' Sasha said. 'I was right behind him, but then I arrived here, and there was nothing.'

A skateboarder skidded to a halt beside them. 'Are you looking for a bad-tempered guy in a shiny suit?' he asked, speaking English.

They all spoke at once:

'Yes!'

'Have you seen him?'

'Where did he go?'

'He went in there,' said the skateboarder, a skinny boy with floppy black hair, pointing to a door of heavy, dark wood. 'Not your dad, is he? He shoved Vigo off his skateboard.'

Maxine shook her head, pulling out her phone. 'He's a crook,' she said. 'We're going to call the police.'

'I'm texting Danny now,' said John, tapping rapidly. 'That's it – done.' Seconds later, his phone pinged a message back and he looked at the screen. 'He's on his way,' he said. 'And he's called the cops. I'm looking forward to this. You guys should stay and watch,' he told the skateboarder.

'Er, no thanks,' the boy replied, signalling to the others. 'The police don't like us much. Glad we could help, though.'

The rumble of skateboards faded down an alleyway, and a few minutes later Danny entered the square from a street on the far side and looked around for them. Maxine gave a wave and he hurried over to join them.

'Are you sure it was him?' he asked. 'We'll look kind of stupid if not.'

'It was him, all right,' said Sasha. 'We saw the boxes of shoes. Listen, here they come.'

They heard the sound of sirens, and two police cars screeched into the square. The doors flew open and uniformed officers spilled onto the street. Danny walked over and addressed them in fluent Spanish. The officers listened for a moment, then they rang the bell. A pale, startled-looking woman opened the door and the police pushed past her and raced up the stairs. Shortly afterwards they emerged, ushering a handcuffed, grim-faced man in front of them. A leather-jacketed detective followed, holding the carrier bag full of shoe boxes. He crossed the street and exchanged a few words with Danny, then jumped into the car and drove off.

Danny turned to them with a huge smile on his face. 'They had to take the shoes for evidence,' he said. 'But that's OK. When this story comes out it'll mean the end for Flame. I reckon Galactic are going to be kind of pleased with you guys, even if you did nearly give me a heart attack, disappearing like that. Who spotted him first?'

'It was Maxine,' said Jade.

'And Sasha was the one who chased after him,' said Maxine.

'High five!' said Danny, slapping their hands. 'I reckon you guys have just saved Camp Gold.' He looked at his watch. 'I'll just text Michael and give him the good news! But then you'd better go and show the world what Camp Gold students can do. And I've thought of a neat way to get us to the stadium. This should be a real treat!'

CHAPTER FIFTEEN

They travelled a few stations on the metro and emerged near the harbour, where Danny led them down a street towards a tower built of metal girders. As they walked down the street Maxine noticed a lift rising up the centre of the tower, and saw Kerry waiting at the foot with the rest of their group of students.

'It's the cable car,' Danny told them, pausing as a small red cabin left the top of the tower, suspended from thin metal wires, and travelled, swaying slightly, high above the water of the harbour. 'It's the best way to see the city and it'll take us right up onto the hill of Montjuïc where the Olympic Stadium is.'

Beside Maxine, Sasha muttered something inaudible.

'What was that?' Maxine asked her.

'It is nothing,' she replied, looking away.

They joined the rest of their party. Kerry had told them what had happened and Maxine and her friends were instantly surrounded by the other students, all eager to hear the story from them.

'There isn't time for that now,' said Danny, returning from the ticket office and handing out tickets. 'This is my treat, but we have to hurry. There's nobody waiting now so we can all get in one car.'

From the top of the tower the view was

astonishing. They could see the beach and the harbour in one direction and the buildings of the city in the other. Beside Maxine, Sasha was unusually quiet, and when the cable car arrived and they were waved aboard, she gripped Maxine's arm tightly.

'What is it?' asked Maxine as the cable car swayed away from the tower and they looked down through the glass sides of the cabin at the tiny yachts moored in the harbour. 'What's the matter?'

'I do not like heights,' said Sasha from between gritted teeth. Her eyes were tightly shut. 'That cathedral was bad enough, but at least it was made of solid rock. This is horrible.' She opened her eyes briefly, looking at the buildings of the city stretching away towards the dark shapes of the craggy hills, and shuddered.

'But . . . but you're a pole-vaulter,' said Maxine as the others stared at Sasha disbelievingly. 'How can you possibly be scared of heights?' She felt the laughter welling up inside her. She tried to stop it, but she couldn't help herself, and the others around her started laughing too.

'How can you do this?' exclaimed Sasha angrily. 'It is not a joke. Get me out of this terrible thing.'

'It's OK,' said Maxine, stifling her giggles. 'We're arriving, look!' The cable car was approaching another tower and it went inside.

'Good!' said Sasha. 'Let me out.'

But the cable car kept going. 'It doesn't stop here, I'm afraid,' said Danny. 'But don't worry, Sasha. It's only another couple of minutes, and we're over land now.'

Sasha wasn't convinced. She kept her eyes shut throughout the journey as the others gazed through the windows at the panorama around them, and she was the first off when the doors opened.

'Why did you ever start pole-vaulting?' asked Maxine as they walked through ornamental gardens and then along a tree-lined road, with glimpses of the city below them through the trees.

'Did you see a big foam landing pad underneath that . . . thing?' asked Sasha. 'Pole-vault is not the same at all. You do not fall onto rocks or into freezing water. Pole-vault is like flying.'

'It is when you do it,' said Maxine. 'I wouldn't dare.'

'There it is,' said Danny, pointing ahead to a series of white walls behind the trees. 'The Olympic Stadium. We'll go round to the front and meet Michael and Isabel. You'll be amazed!'

They went down several flights of steps and came out into a wide open space where rows of yellow pillars made an avenue that led towards the city. People were flooding up the steps from the city below, heading for the impressive entrance of the stadium. At the edge of the plaza, a white tower rose into the sky, and beneath it they saw Michael and Isabel waiting for them. They were both smiling.

'You guys have probably saved Camp Gold,' Michael said with a huge grin. 'Quick eyes and quick thinking, by the sound of it. I think Galactic are sensing big publicity from all this, but I've asked them not to announce anything until tomorrow. You need to be able to concentrate on this event. Are you ready? You're up first, Sasha – the pole-vault events are among the first to go.'

He led the way to the changing rooms, where they found their bags waiting for them. As soon as they walked inside Maxine felt the nerves hit her. She also felt tired as she sat down on a bench beside Jade and Hiari; she sat back and closed her eyes for a moment. It had been a long and exciting day and it seemed like weeks since they had woken to discover the break-in. Now they were here in the Olympic Stadium, in the very changing rooms where Olympic champions had prepared themselves to win their medals.

She stole a glance at Hiari and Jade. Were they as nervous as she was? They were her friends, but for the next two hours she had to try to put that out of her mind. At the end of the evening someone would have won the right to carry the Olympic torch – but only one. Her phone buzzed in her pocket. It was a text from her mum: **Good luck!!!! Joshua says make sure you win!!! X**

She looked at the others again. Three weeks ago she knew she would have had no chance of beating them, but now – now she knew she could run as fast as them. There was only a tenth of a second between them all. It would all come down to who was the most focused, the most relaxed, and who got their tactics right.

Maxine changed, and went off by herself into the warm-up area. As she went through her stretches, she tried to visualize the race as she wanted it to be. Hiari would run from the front. She always did. And Jade would track her every step of the way, relying on her grit and courage to take her through the pain. I mustn't get sucked into a fight between them, Maxine told herself. I'll run it at my own pace. I'll take them right at the end.

She held the image in her mind. The finish line was in sight; the other two were ahead but she was closing fast. She passed them right on the line. She was going to make it happen.

Maxine looked up and saw that Kerry had joined her in the warm-up area, doing her own sequence of stretches and beginning to focus on her own battle against her rivals.

'You're looking good,' Kerry said. 'Are you

going to watch your friends first? The junior pole-vault is just starting, and the four hundred metres goes in ten minutes. You have plenty of time. My race is first, and then yours, but it's not for an hour.' She lunged into a series of calf stretches – and suddenly Kerry, the friend, was gone and Kerry, the serious athlete, was back in business.

Kath was next to join them and she gathered the junior 800-metre runners and took them through a maze of corridors and then through a passageway into the stadium itself. As they came out onto the side of the track a roar went up from the crowd, and against the background of thousands of faces Maxine saw Sasha rise into the air and float over the pole-vault bar. Ripples of applause ran around the stadium as Sasha's leap was replayed on the giant screens at either end.

'This way,' said Kath, and a steward held open

a gate to let them into a section of the stand reserved for the Camp Gold contingent. As they took their seats Maxine was able to see the size of the crowd properly for the first time. Every seat in the stadium was taken and there was a buzz of expectation as the athletes moved onto the track for the elite 400 metres race.

They took up their positions and the announcer introduced them to the crowd. 'It's almost the same line-up as it was for the World Championships,' Kath told them. 'Danny won that, of course, with Darren Wilkins a close second, but there's a Chinese guy who was right up there with them too. That's him there. Ho Feng. He's drawn the outside lane, though. I doubt if he can win it from there.'

But she was wrong. Ho Feng got a brilliant start, and despite the stagger he appeared to be gaining on the athletes inside him. He was still a metre clear of Darren Wilkins as they came into the final straight, and although Wilkins nearly caught him in a finish that had the crowd on its feet, Ho Feng held on to win.

As the crowd noise subsided, the junior 400 metres was announced. Maxine saw John walking onto the track and suddenly she was trembling with nerves for him. It was worse than any worries she'd ever had for herself.

'It's OK,' said Jade, beside her. 'He looks . . . well, he looks kind of grown up. He looks ready.'

It was true, Maxine thought, as she watched John move to his position in lane four. He seemed to have actually grown in the three weeks they'd been at Camp Gold. He looked taller; he was lean and muscular, and there was a fiercely determined expression on his face. Suddenly a voice from the crowd behind them called out, 'Go on, John. You can do it!'

Maxine recognized Rosalita's voice and, looking up, saw her waving madly. Down on the track John's concentration broke for a second as he smiled and gave a brief wave back. Then his face became a mask once more.

The starting pistol cracked and John exploded out of the blocks. From his very first stride Maxine had no doubt that he was going to win the race. And he didn't just win; he totally destroyed the rest of the field. As he thundered down the final straight he was five metres clear of his nearest challenger, but he didn't let his pace slacken until he crossed the line. He punched the air as he looked up at the giant screen, and flung his arms skywards when he saw that the time was a record for his age group.

The noise of the crowd was immense, and Maxine realized that she was on her feet, cheering with the rest of them. 'Wow!' exclaimed Kerry behind her. 'That was awesome! That boy is going to be a champion. There is no doubt about that!' She looked at her watch. 'Time for me to go,' she said. 'I have half an hour.'

Kath checked her own watch, gathered the Camp Gold 800-metre runners together and they followed Kerry back over to the call room.

Once there, Maxine watched the elite runners warming up. She had seen them all on TV, but it was different being so close to a whole group of athletes who were at the very top in her own event. Feluke Okoye, the world record holder, was warming up just a few metres away. The runners were called for their race and Maxine knew better than to call out encouragement to Kerry. From the moment they had arrived in the call room, Kerry had entered a closed, private world again, just like the rest of the competitors.

They moved out onto the track and Maxine and her friends turned to watch the race. The crowd hushed in anticipation of another titanic struggle.

'On your marks . . .'

The sound of the gun echoed around the stadium, the crowd roared and the athletes were sprinting round the first bend. As they came together after breaking for the inside lane, there was some bumping and jostling. Maxine saw Kerry stumble briefly, and suddenly she was at the back of the field.

'It's OK,' said Hiari. 'They are bunched up tight. She'll take them all.'

The field stayed close together until they came round to take the bell, but as they entered the back straight with 300 metres to go, Feluke Okoye made a move. Stretching out her legs, she sprinted into a three-metre lead. For a moment, Maxine thought she would continue to move away from the rest, but a group of three went with her, preventing the gap from growing larger, and Kerry was running comfortably at the back of that group. As they entered the final straight Kerry moved to the outside, and with an irresistible surge of power she motored past the two women in front of her. There was only the world record holder to catch now, and Maxine could see that Feluke Okoye was worried. She glanced over her shoulder, and that glance gave Kerry all the encouragement she needed. The two runners crossed the line together, but when the replay appeared on the screens it was clear that Kerry had won the race.

The crowd stood to applaud the victory, but then, as the time appeared on the screen, there was a brief, disbelieving hush. The letters *WR* were flashing in red beside the time. Kerry Jones had broken the world record! The applause grew into a vast noise that echoed around the arena as Kerry jogged round a lap of honour.

Maxine was cheering like the rest, but then she turned and saw that Jade had turned white. She was biting her lip and she seemed to be talking to herself. Reality hit Maxine like a fist in the stomach. In five minutes, her own race would begin. It hadn't seemed real until now. The crowd, the stadium – they were for someone else, not for her. But soon they would be calling out her name. She shivered and felt instinctively for her wrist – then froze with horror.

Joshua's bracelet!

It wasn't there!

CHAPTER SIXTEEN

'Maxine! Where are you going?' Jade was staring at her in amazement.

Maxine stopped and turned back for a second. 'My bracelet,' she said. 'I took it off when I was changing. We were in such a hurry to get out and see John run that I forgot to put it on again.'

'But you can't! There isn't time.'

The other girls had all stopped warming up and were staring at Maxine in horror. Maxine turned and ran back through the corridors. There was no way she could run without Johsua's bracelet on her arm. She dashed into the changing room and saw it lying there on the bench where she had left it. She picked it up and slipped it onto her wrist, thinking of Joshua's message: *Make sure you win*.

She heard the boom of the announcer's voice, but couldn't make out the words. She raced back down the corridor and out into the waiting area, but it was empty. She stared around in a panic, and then saw the back of Hui Zhong's head walking away from her along the side of the track. She took a deep breath and followed, telling herself not to rush, aware that her heart was beating far too fast.

As she reached the start, the other runners were already taking their positions. Hiari had been drawn in lane one, and she was standing there, shaking her hands by her side in a characteristic gesture, staring straight ahead of her as if she couldn't see the crowd at all. Outside her was the Canadian girl, Jerry, and then Hui Zhong. Martha, the Californian girl, was in lane four, and Estrella, the Argentinian, in lane five.

Then there was an empty lane. Lane six. Maxine's lane.

Lane seven was Yuriko, the quiet Japanese girl. Yuriko was a mystery. None of Maxine's friends had really managed to get to know her. She had kept herself to herself and slipped in and out of training like a slim – though powerful and increasingly fast – little sprite.

As she walked up to the line Maxine saw Jade, who was in lane eight, glance back and give the briefest of nods in her direction. Then she heard the sound of slow handclapping from the far side of the track and looked over to see Sasha standing on the pole-vault runway, rocking back and forth as the claps came faster and faster.

Then Sasha was away and running. She planted her pole and twisted upwards, clearing the bar with only millimetres to spare. As the applause rang out, the announcer began to introduce the 800-metre runners. Maxine smiled to herself. Sasha's bad dreams had not come true, and it was obvious that her shaky moments in the cable car hadn't done her any harm. She heard Sasha's voice in her head: *I always believe that I am going to win.*

Maxine repeated the words over and over to herself: *I'm going to win. I'm going to win.*

Hiari was waving to the crowd now as her name rang out. Maxine looked down at the ground. Hiari would run from the front. I won't go with her, Maxine reminded herself. I'm going to run this at my own pace and take her at the end, just like Kerry Jones did with Feluke Okoye.

And now it was her own name that was

booming around the stadium: '*In lane six, Maxine Fula.*'

She raised a hand self-consciously and heard warm applause in response. The final two runners were introduced, and then a hush fell over the stadium.

'On your marks . . .'

Maxine stepped forward and crouched, every muscle in her body tensed to respond.

'*Crack!*'

The pistol fired and they were away. Maxine focused her attention on Jade, two lanes outside her. More than any of the others, Jade seemed to have her own personal clock inside her head. She would make no mistake with the pace. Maxine passed Yuriko in lane seven. The immense noise of the crowd seemed to fade away and all she could hear was the thud of feet on the track, and the sound of breathing. She sensed that Martha and Estrella on the inside were tracking her closely – they always seemed to run as a pair, and she knew she'd have to watch out for them when she broke for the pole position.

As they approached that point, she risked a glance across to her inside and saw Hiari accelerating smoothly up the inside lane, determined to run the race from the front. They broke from their lanes, and at once Maxine had to make a decision: sprint hard to pass in front of Estrella and Martha and tuck in behind Hiari, or let them go, keeping her rhythm and sacrificing her position.

She let them go. She felt good, and in a race like this it was better to stay out of trouble. When she saw Martha collide with Hui Zhong, forcing the Chinese girl to stumble, she knew that she had made the right decision. Both Hui Zhong and the American lost a couple of metres and Maxine settled in behind Estrella, Jade and Hiari.

It was going to be OK. The race was going

exactly as she had visualized it. She'd avoided the worst of the hurly-burly as they'd broken for the inside, and now she relaxed, but even as she was congratulating herself on the best start she'd had for ages, she realized that something was wrong.

The pace was fast, she knew that. She hadn't expected anything else. But suddenly she saw that Hiari had opened up a significant gap. She was two metres ahead of Jade, and still moving away from her, as if she was accelerating all the time. Let her go, she told herself. She can't keep this up.

But this was Hiari. Maxine had never seen Hiari tie up at the end of a race. Not once. Not ever.

She felt the doubt growing in her and she was in an agony of indecision. Another five seconds and it would be too late. Hiari must believe she can do it, Maxine told herself. And if she can, I'll never catch her.

Her decision was made. As they approached the bend she moved out and passed Estrella, who gave her a brief, startled glance. Jade sensed her presence, and as Maxine went past her she felt the other girl respond. Hiari was three metres ahead, but with her decision made Maxine put in a huge effort to catch her. It felt as if she was sprinting for the finish line, but that was still more than a lap away.

Now Hiari was only two metres ahead. She had to catch her. She knew if she made the attempt and failed, the race would be as good as over. But Hiari was still driving on at the same searing pace and it took fierce determination and persistence on Maxine's part to keep chipping away at those remaining two metres until, at last, she was within touching distance again.

They were coming off the bend now, into the home straight. The effort of catching Hiari had drained Maxine, but she kept her legs pounding forward and slowly she recovered her poise. She was breathing easily and she felt as if Hiari was pulling her along. But then, as they approached the bell, everything seemed to happen at once.

Hiari was running away from her again. Her concentration had flickered for a split second, and in that brief moment a gap had opened. Even as she fought to respond she felt Jade slip past on her outside. At the same moment the bell was ringing and Maxine sensed that the rest of the field were closing up behind her. She glanced over her shoulder and, sure enough, Hui Zhong was leading a group of runners who seemed to be catching her fast.

Glancing back had been a mistake. She knew that at once, and as she focused again on the track ahead of her she saw that Hiari and Jade had opened up a clear gap. They were way ahead of her and the gap was growing with every stride.

She fought to control her panic. This race was now nothing like the one she had visualized beforehand. Only one thing was the same: Hiari was dominating from the front, and there was nothing she could do about that. Time seemed to slow as she forced herself to keep going.

Her chances were looking increasingly hopeless with every stride. But then she remembered all the cold winter nights at the track, running and running when all her friends were out having a good time. She remembered the struggle to get her schoolwork done when training was over, and the times when she had failed and trouble had followed.

It had all been for nothing, and now she was going to be humiliated in front of fifty thousand people because she had made all the wrong decisions yet again.

Maybe she shouldn't have gone back for the bracelet. Maybe that was where the trouble had started. She looked down and there it was, glittering on her wrist.

Make sure you win! Joshua had said.

Well, that wasn't going to happen now. Hiari was a natural. Maxine thought of her running all that way to school and back, every day of her young life. Running was in her blood.

And Jade – nobody had determination like Jade's. There was no way she was going to catch them.

Maxine felt tears pricking her eyes, heard the pounding feet of the rest of the field closing on her, and wished fervently that she was anywhere but here.

CHAPTER SEVENTEEN

Suddenly a voice cut through the noise of the crowd.

'Go on, Maxine, you can still catch them! Remember the sunrise!'

It was Kerry Jones. She was standing behind a barrier in the area reserved for the elite athletes, with a flag still draped around her shoulders from her victory celebrations. Maxine caught just a glimpse of Kerry passionately urging her on, but that glimpse was enough.

In the midst of all the noise and intensity, she closed her eyes for a second and was back on the mountain trail at dawn, breathing the clean air and the scent of the pine trees.

She opened her eyes again. Joshua's bracelet glowed in the floodlights, just as it had done in the first rays of the rising sun. The gap was still the same. The other runners were no closer to catching her. She had made mistakes, sure, but even so she was still in with a chance in the biggest race of her life. She was feeling good, she was running well, and maybe Kerry was right.

Maybe she could still win.

They were off the bend now, and into the back straight of the second and final lap. Hiari was running with her usual fluid motion and Maxine remembered running beside her, back from the fiesta in the dusk. She had run a long way that night. She had been tired, but she had still kept pace with Hiari. If she could do it then, she could do it now.

It was the noise from the crowd that gave her the first clue that she might be gaining on the two girls in front of her. And then she heard Sasha's voice as she passed the pole-vault runway.

'Go, Maxine! You are catching them!'

At the sound of Sasha's voice, Jade looked back over her shoulder and the slightly jerky rhythm of her running was interrupted for a split second. Long enough for Maxine to edge half a metre closer to her and for Hiari to open up clear space between her and Jade.

Now Maxine could hear the sound of Jade's breathing, but Jade refused to allow Hiari to get away from her, and with her usual grit she closed the gap again. Maxine stayed with Jade; in touch, but only just. She knew she couldn't afford to let the gap grow again, but she was hurting now. Every breath was searing her lungs, the muscles in her legs were on fire and a nagging pain was growing in her side.

All round the final bend the three girls ran in single file, Hiari in the lead, Jade running in her footsteps and Maxine a metre and a half behind Jade.

A metre and a half.

It was too far.

Maxine knew the gap was too big. Much better if she were right on Jade's heels, ready to pounce. Every nerve ending in her body seemed to be screaming at her in protest, but still she kept forcing herself forwards as the noise of the crowd grew to a crescendo.

They were in the straight now. Just a hundred metres left to run. Maxine moved out to her right. She was closing on Jade, she was sure of it! Centimetre by centimetre she was creeping closer, and at the same time Jade was closing on Hiari. The knowledge that she was actually gaining on Jade gave Maxine a new burst of energy. Stride by painful stride she drew closer.

The three girls were almost in a line now, and the crowd was on its feet. Hiari still led, with Jade fractionally behind her and Maxine gaining all the time. Maxine knew that she could take them both, but could she do it before they reached the finish line? Her arm came up and the bracelet glittered in the floodlights. She heard Joshua's voice in her head:

You have to win!

She hurled herself forward towards the line. She was dimly aware of the other two doing the same thing beside her, dimly aware of the roar of the crowd as the three athletes flashed across the line, seemingly at exactly the same moment, and then she was stumbling and collapsing to the ground as her legs gave way beneath her.

When she finally looked up, she saw Hiari

crouched on the track nearby. Jade was lying flat on her back and the crowd was still cheering loudly. Kath appeared at Maxine's side.

'Who won?' Maxine asked, her voice coming out as a hoarse croak.

Kath shook her head. 'Impossible to tell,' she said, helping Maxine to her feet. 'We're waiting for the photo. Look, there's a replay.'

Hiari pulled Jade upright, and together they watched the final hundred metres replayed on the massive screens at each end of the stadium. As they approached the line there was nothing to choose between the three of them. Maxine was definitely overtaking the other two, but it was quite impossible to see if she had succeeded. Then they saw the finish again, this time from the side.

'It's a tie,' said Maxine. 'It must be.'

'Wait,' said Kath. 'Here comes the result.'

The noise of the crowd died suddenly as the words flashed up on the board.

Maxine's eyes blurred with tears. She couldn't read the rest.

'You all finished in the same time,' Kath yelled in her ear above the roar of the crowd. 'They couldn't separate Hiari and Jade, but you were a fraction ahead. Well done, Maxine! Well done, all of you! That was just magnificent!'

Hiari and Jade both hugged Maxine, and they stood with their arms around each other's shoulders, waving up at the crowd. The other runners came up and congratulated them and Maxine was astonished to see that everyone in the crowd nearby was standing. The applause just seemed to grow and grow.

'You should all run a lap of honour,' Kath prompted them. 'Go on. You've earned it.'

The girls set off, jogging round the edge of

the track, and as they went they saw people everywhere standing and cheering. They were approaching the pole-vault area when Maxine saw Sasha waving at her.

'Look!' cried Sasha, pointing. 'Up there in the stand!'

Maxine looked, and at first she couldn't believe her eyes. High up to her right she saw her mum, standing up and waving madly with one arm while she held firmly onto Joshua, who was sitting precariously on her shoulders and yelling at the top of his voice. Her dad was there too, and her big sister, Lola, and Kayle, her oldest, best friend, leaping up and down and punching the air.

Maxine lifted her arm and pointed to the shiny bracelet on her wrist, then blew a kiss to her family and her friend. She felt as if she was floating as she continued her journey round the stadium. And then, as they arrived back at the finish, Kath pointed out the cluster of cameramen and reporters waiting beside the track.

'The TV people want to speak to you first,' she said. 'Then they'll all want to take photos and ask you some questions.'

'Do we have to?' asked Maxine nervously. She felt exhausted now, and just wanted to get back to the changing room.

Kath smiled. 'You're going to be famous,' she said. 'You might as well get used to it.'

The girls were ushered into an enclosure and Maxine blinked at the dazzling TV lights and the persistent flash of cameras. Then she saw that Michael, Danny and Isabel were waiting there too, already speaking to the tall, suntanned interviewer.

'We've brought together these fine young athletes from all over the world,' Michael said. 'And you can see for yourselves what we've achieved together. Maxine, Hiari, Jade, over here.' He beckoned to the girls and they joined him in front of the camera.

'How does it feel to win a race like that in front of such a fantastic crowd?' the interviewer asked Maxine.

'It was awesome,' she replied. 'I didn't think I'd ever catch them. I wasn't even sure if I had. I mean, if it hadn't been somewhere like this with the computers and cameras, everyone would have said it was a tie.'

'It was a wonderful fight-back. Up in the commentary box we were all sure you'd never make it.' The interviewer turned to Hiari. 'I guess you thought so too?'

'I know how good my friends are,' replied Hiari. 'We all tried our best and Maxine was just too good for us today. Maybe next time it will be different.'

'Well, one thing's for sure,' the interviewer

said. 'We'll be seeing an awful lot more
of all three of you in the future. But tell me,
Maxine, how does it feel to know you'll be
carrying the Olympic torch through your home
town?'

'It's . . . it's really cool,' said Maxine. But even
as she said it she felt bad, seeing the
disappointment that flickered across the faces of
Jade and Hiari.

The interviewer signed off, and Michael,
Isabel and Danny took the girls to talk to
reporters. Maxine answered all their questions
and tried hard to keep smiling, but all the time
she was feeling sad for her friends. They had all
finished in the same time, and it didn't seem fair
that she was the only one who'd be carrying the
torch. They would all have another chance to
beat each other in races in the future, but there
was only one chance to carry that torch and she
knew how they must be feeling.

'I'm sorry,' she said to the others as they changed.

'Don't be,' replied Jade. 'We always knew that only one of us could be the winner, and it was you. So what if it was only millimetres?'

'Yes,' agreed Hiari, 'and anyway, I'm planning to win an Olympic gold medal. That's going to be even better than carrying the torch.'

'Hey!' said Jade, her eyes shining. 'Maybe we'll have another race like that one day – in the Olympic final.'

'Maybe you will,' said Kath, coming into the changing room, 'but right now I think you should all come and watch the pole-vault final. Your friend, Sasha, has one vault left to make.'

They hurried outside and Kath escorted them round the perimeter of the track. They arrived just in time to see Sasha stripping off her tracksuit. 'Diane has failed three times at this height,' Kath told them, 'and this is Sasha's final attempt. If she clears it she'll be the winner.'

'I bet she will,' said John, rushing up as the friends entered the athletes' enclosure. 'That was the most awesome race I've ever seen, you guys! Incredible. You were all winners. And Sasha will be too, just watch.'

Sasha was going through her routine at the far end of the runway, and the friends joined in as the spectators began to clap. The clapping speeded up and grew louder and louder, then fell suddenly silent as Sasha sprinted down the runway. The pole crunched into the box, the pole bent into an impossible curve and then straightened, catapulting Sasha high into the air, up . . . and over the bar!

She landed on the pad, bounced once and jumped up with her arms raised high in triumph as the stadium erupted in noise.

'Can you believe it?' said Maxine. 'This has been the best day ever!'

But the day was not over yet. When the competition was finished Maxine met her family outside the stadium. Joshua ran over to her, yelling, 'You did it! You did it!' and she lifted him up and hugged him.

'It was my bracelet that did it, right?' he asked her, and she smiled.

'Definitely,' she replied. 'That and me running very fast. But what are you all doing here? How did you get here?'

'We drove,' said her dad, ruffling her hair. 'That old car is not finished yet, you know. And we borrowed a tent and camped on the way. We even brought Kayle. Pretty cool, huh!'

Maxine stared at her mum and dad in disbelief. They had never camped in their lives. Then she felt her eyes filling with tears. They had done it so that they could watch her run. They had come all this way! They had slept in a tent! She hugged them all again.

'We are going for a meal,' her mum said. 'We're going to celebrate. Can you come?'

'I . . . I don't know. I'd like to but—'

'Maxine, are you ready? We have to go inside.' It was Kath. Maxine had told the coach that her parents were here, and she'd allowed her a few minutes to meet them.

'I'm sorry,' Maxine said. 'There's a big party inside and we all have to be there.'

'No, wait,' said Kath, looking at the disappointed faces. 'Let me call Michael.' She turned away as she dialled, had a short conversation, then turned back to them, smiling. 'Michael says that, without Maxine, Camp Gold would probably be finished, so you're all very welcome to join us. OK?'

'Yes!' cried Joshua. 'A party. Is there food?'

'Sure,' said Kath, laughing. 'Excellent food. All you can eat. Let's go.'

The party was thrilling. All the elite athletes

were there, and all the students from Camp Gold International, but Maxine had to spend a lot of time explaining to her family just what had been going on there during the past three weeks. By the time she had finished, Michael was ready to make a speech.

'The last few weeks have been just a little too exciting,' he said. 'It seems to me that whenever Sasha, John, Jade and Maxine get together there's always some kind of trouble.' He paused while everyone laughed. 'However,' he continued, 'this time they didn't cause the trouble – or not much of it, anyway.'

'What did he mean by that?' asked Maxine's dad.

'Be quiet,' said her mum. 'Just listen!'

'Things never seem to run smoothly at Camp Gold,' Michael said. 'But I wouldn't have missed it for the world. Look at the great performances we've seen today, from every one of you. And look at the fantastic commitment that every athlete has shown – even those of you who weren't selected to run today. Trust me, your time will come!'

There was loud applause at this.

'Camp Gold is a new idea,' Michael went on. 'This is only its second year, and the first for Camp Gold International. But I can tell you now that, thanks to the hard work from all of you here, we have funding for years to come. All we need now is for our first Camp Gold graduate to win an Olympic gold medal. It could even be one of you standing right here this evening.'

There was more loud cheering. Michael's words went straight to Maxine's heart. After her victory today she knew that anything was possible. It could actually happen.

One day, if she worked hard, if nothing went wrong, she could be the one.

She could win Olympic gold.

Then she looked at Hiari and Jade, both standing nearby. Their shining eyes met. And Maxine knew.

They were all thinking exactly the same thing!

Winning Olympic gold was never going to be easy!

NINE MONTHS LATER

Maxine Fula, dressed in running vest, shorts and
brand-new Galactic Meganova running shoes,
was waiting at the roadside to receive the
Olympic torch. The sun was beating down on a
hot afternoon and crowds were lining the streets.
There were whole classes of schoolchildren, all
waving flags. Maxine saw her little brother Joshua
with his classmates and gave him a nervous wave.
She was still wearing the glittery bracelet that

had brought her luck in every race she had run since that evening in the Olympic Stadium.

Nervous flutters ran through Maxine's stomach. She felt more nervous than she'd been before any of the races she had run, and won, since that famous day in Barcelona. She had been having bad dreams about dropping the torch and the flame going out. It would be so awful if that happened. The worst thing ever. It would be replayed on TV and YouTube a million times.

Maxine wished that Sasha was here, with her invincible confidence. Sasha hadn't dropped the torch. Her turn had come a week ago. She had carried the torch through her home town in Russia, and Maxine and Kayle had watched together on the Internet as she had jogged down a wide avenue lined with tall apartment blocks. She had handed over the torch to the next runner beneath an enormous statue in a very grand square with a band playing. The very same torch was now on its way to Maxine.

There was a stir in the crowd and Maxine heard cheering and clapping in the distance. The torch was on its way and the TV cameramen checked their equipment and focused their cameras on the street corner where the runner would appear.

There was a shout from further down the road and Maxine heard someone call her name. She turned and saw Danny Crowe coming towards her. There was someone with him, her arm linked through his. Kerry Jones.

'Hi, Maxine,' they said together.

'We came to wish you luck,' Kerry said. 'Isn't it great about the others?'

'Yes,' said Maxine. 'I don't know how Michael did it. It's fantastic.'

They had heard the news the month before. Michael had persuaded the authorities that all three of the 800-metre runners should be allowed to carry the torch, and Maxine had watched on TV as Hiari had carried it along the route she had taken as a child from her tiny village to her school. Tomorrow it would be Jade's turn, and Maxine was going to travel with her family to watch the event in the northern town where Jade lived.

Danny and Kerry turned away to greet Maxine's parents and family, who were waiting nearby.

'Awesome,' breathed Kayle. 'Do you think they're really together? Or are they just friends?'

'I don't know,' replied Maxine, glad to have something to take her mind off the approaching torch.

A small crowd of photographers had gathered around the couple. Kerry smiled, looked at Danny and then kissed him. 'There,' she said. 'Does that answer your questions? Take some pictures and then get on with your real job. The

Olympic torch is what you're here for, right?'

'And Maxine Fula, of course,' said Danny, giving the cameras his most charming smile. 'Maxine is a star of the future.' Maxine felt herself blushing as the cameras turned back towards her.

'There he is!' someone called out, and every head turned to look down the street to where, two hundred metres away, a teenager in a streamlined wheelchair had rolled into sight.

The cheering followed him down the street. He came fast, powering the chair with one hand, and with the other holding the torch high in the air. He was going so fast that the flame flickered and Maxine worried for a moment that it might be blown out. But as he slowed down for the handover the flame burned brightly again. Maxine readied herself, stepped forward, and in a blaze of camera flashes took the torch from the boy's hands and held it high.

Maxine looked around one last time. She saw her family and friends, her dad beaming proudly with his huge arm around her mum's shoulders. She saw Danny and Kerry, watching and cheering with beaming smiles on their faces. She saw Joshua and his friends, all waving their flags and holding up painted Olympic torches they had made at school.

They had all helped her to get here, to set off on this journey.

Maxine ran.

She ran down the streets lined with cheering people, wondering where her journey was going to take her, and hoping . . . hoping that her journey would end in gold.

ABOUT THE AUTHOR

When Christine was fifteen years old, at her school sports day, she tried the 800 metres for the first time. Back then, she and her brother and sisters were always trying to outdo each other on sports days – they all wanted to be able to tell their parents that they had won an event. On this particular sports day, Christine ran the 800 metres – and won! She was chuffed to be able to come home as a winner. Nobody realized that this was only the start of her winning streak.

At the age of sixteen, Christine joined the Newham and Essex Beagles Athletics Club and her talent for running was instantly recognized.

Although she was already playing netball for England she was told that she would be better off concentrating on athletics. The Newham and Essex Beagles coaches could see straight away that Christine had amazing talent. She had no training, but was beating girls who had been running for years. Sometimes she trained with the boys because she was so fast!

Christine won gold in the 400 metres at the Beijing Olympics in 2008 and is part of Team GB's Olympic squad for the London 2012 Olympics.

In 2009 she was awarded an MBE in the New Year's Honours list.

NOW IS THE TIME FOR RUNNING

On the dusty fields of Zimbabwe, Deo and Innocent
are playing football. Then the soldiers come looking
for food and traitors — destroying the only home
the boys have ever known. Now they have nothing
but each other, and a football stuffed with billions of
worthless dollars. And so starts a journey of a lifetime,
to find safety with a father they have never met. But
with soldiers everywhere, they have only one chance
to cross the border, one chance to escape.
Now is the time for courage.
Now is the time for running.

Gripping, suspenseful and deeply
compassionate – *Kirkus Review*

ISBN: 978 1 848 53083 6

SPORTING HEROES

What does an Olympic champion eat for breakfast?
How can you become the fastest runner in the
world? At what age can you start training to
be a boxer?

Interesting facts, super secrets and never seen photos
of some of the best-known sporting heroes including
boxer Amir Khan, runners Mo Farah & Christine
Ohuruogu, basketball sensation Luol Deng and the
gymnast Louis Smith, who has been tipped
for 2012 success.

Look inside for tips on how to get into sports, where
you can train, and how you too can become
a sporting hero.

ISBN: 978 1 848 53097 3